ABBA ABBA

ABBA ABBA

Anthony Burgess

FOREWORD BY MICHAEL DIRDA

BARNES & NOBLE

NEW YORK

To Liana

Barnes & Noble, Inc.
122 Fifth Avenue
New York, NY 10011

ISBN: 978-1-4351-0423-5

Printed and bound in the United States of America

10 9 8 7 6 5 4 3 2 1

FOREWORD

LIKE SO MUCH OF ANTHONY BURGESS'S WORK, *ABBA ABBA* doesn't fit easily into any single genre. It opens with a novella-length re-creation of John Keats's last days in Rome, as the dying twenty-five-year-old spits up blood, discusses art and poetry with friends, and daydreams about sex, love, and the poems he will never write. This is followed by a short section, describing the later careers of Keats's friend Joseph Severn, his doctor James Clark, and the Roman-dialect poet Giuseppe Belli. The last forty pages of *ABBA ABBA* offer a selection from one J. J. Wilson's "draft translations" of Belli's sonnets on Biblical subjects. Thus, in less than 150 pages, Burgess packs together fiction, nonfiction, and poetry. His title, furthermore, neatly alludes to Christ's dying cry from the cross ("*Abba, Abba,*" that is, the Aramaic words for "Father, Father"), the rhyme scheme of the opening octet in a Petrarchan sonnet, and the initials of the book's author.

Though best known for *A Clockwork Orange*, Burgess was astonishingly prolific. In nearly four decades of tireless activity, he produced a couple of dozen novels (most of them comic and at least somewhat experimental in form); several verse dramas and film scripts; a children's book; a great deal of literary journalism; and a number of semi-scholarly books about linguistics, James Joyce, and music. Despite its variety, all this disparate work is nonetheless recognizably from the same typewriter. Burgess's style is always slightly artificial, musical, and fancy enough to require the aid of an unabridged dictionary; his sentences are tight and compact, oddly structured, and vaguely Joycean in the frequent use of fragments. Just as one reads Agatha Christie for the tricksiness of her plots, so one picks up any book by Anthony Burgess for the baroque richness and crackle of the prose, the restlessly sprightly tone, the non-stop energy and exuberance of the narrative voice. The patter and playfulness never stop; the man is half strutting showman, half Shakespeare. Readers don't lose themselves in a Burgess story; they just sit back and enjoy one of the great performance artists of the English language.

In *ABBA ABBA* this virtuoso writer stuffs his novella with literary allusions (e.g., to the *Edinburgh Review*'s vicious putdown of Keats's poetry: "This will never do"), illustrates the importance and vitality of dialects such as Roman and Scotch (*vs.* Tuscan Italian and standard English), discusses Elizabethan pronunciation, and revels in blasphemy and elegant bawdry and clever wordplay ("Keats takes steak"). When the feverish poet describes to Severn an (imaginary) night with the naked Pauline Bonaparte, he adopts a deliberately luscious and anti- quated English reminiscent of Robert Burton's *The Anatomy of Mel- ancholy*: "She instructed me in all of the modes of physical possession out of her deep learning. Marry, I cannot remember the names of them all, but there was certes the pavonian touch, the Ledan straddle too, the chthonian ditch, the I think it was termed Ceutan flight and eke the Madrilenan interuberal. . . . ."

While the novella portion of *ABBA ABBA* may be enjoyed as an elegant and even erudite conversation piece—like the dialogue novels of Thomas Love Peacock or the early comedies of Aldous Huxley—the section devoted to Belli's Roman-dialect sonnets possesses an earthier appeal. (Translator J. J. Wilson bears more than a passing resemblance to the man born John Anthony Burgess Wilson.) Belli wrote more than 2,000 of these witty and satirical, colloquial and immensely readable poems. Here's just the octet to "Annunciation": *You know the day, the month, even the year./While Mary ate her noonday plate of soup,/ The Angel Gabriel, like a heaven-hurled hoop,/Was bowling towards her through the atmosphere./She watched him crash the window with- out fear/And enter through the hole in one swift swoop./A lily in his fist, his wings adroop,/"Ave," he said, and after that, "Maria....*

Anthony Burgess frequently used writers as his protagonists— think of the poet-hero of the four Enderby books, Kenneth Toomey of the Booker-nominated *Earthly Powers*, young Will Shakespeare in *Nothing Like the Sun*. This double homage to poets John Keats and Giuseppe Belli belongs in their company. *ABBA ABBA* may be a slen- der and rather idiosyncratic book, but it is a delightful one too.

—MICHAEL DIRDA
November 2008

ABBA ABBA

*I would reject a petrarchal coronation—on account
of my dying day, and because women have cancers.*

JOHN KEATS

Part One

I

"Isaac," he said. "Marmaduke. Which of the two do you more seem to yourself to be?" He mused smiling among the ilex trees. The dome of San Pietro down there in the city was grape-hued in the citron twilight.

"I have never much cared for either name," said Lieutenant Elton of the Royal Engineers. "At school they called me Ikey Marmalade."

"We're both edibles then. Junkets, me."

"Junkets? Oh yes. Jun Kets."

"To be eaten by Fairy Mab."

Elton did not catch the reference. He took out his handkerchief, coughed harshly into it, then examined the sputum in the lemon dusk. Satisfied with what he saw, he wrapped it and stowed it in his pocket. He said:

"It's the mildness here that is good. The winter will be very mild, you will see. Extremes are bad. On St Helena a raging summer is ready to begin. Not good for the lungs, that climate. Not good for the liver. Not good for anything."

"You spoke with Bony at all?"

"He waved his arms and said something about earthquakes or it may have been earthworks. Or earthworms, for that matter. I could not understand his French very well. I saw him digging a lot. *Il faut cultiver notre jardin,* he shouted at me. That's from the atheist Voltaire."

"You don't admire Voltaire?"

"A damned atheist."

"Here comes his sister."

"Voltaire's?"

"No, no, no. God in heaven, here truly comes his sister. To us."

Pauline Bonaparte glided in the dimming light, a couple of servants behind her, taking her evening walk on the Pincio. Elegant, lovely, with a fine style of countenance of the lengthened sort, fine-nostrilled, fine-eyed, she peered with fine eyes at the taller and more handsome of the two young men, gliding closer to peer better. Elton stood stiffly as though on adjutant's parade, suffering the inspection. She smiled and nodded and glided on. His friend laughed, though nervously.

"Fairy Mab will have you."

"Ah no. Ah no she'll not. I'm no whoremaster."

"Faithful to the one at home?"

"Yes, you could say faithful."

John brooded. "I too. The animal ecstasy of the flesh denied to us. We're not winds to play on that Aeolian Harp."

"What Aeolian Harp?"

"Her as Venus Reclining. Canova's work, apt for the hallway of a whorehouse. To be played on by any wind that blows, gale, zephyr, postcenal eructation." He paused to take in shallow breaths while Elton looked puzzled. "Can they be disjointed, *disjuncted*, disjunketed?"

"What?" They turned, in Pauline's far wake, towards the Spanish Steps.

"Love and the animal ecstasy."

"It is ennobled," said Lieutenant Elton RE, "by love. It ceases to be animal and becomes divine."

"In what bad poet did you read that?"

"I read no poetry. I read only engineering manuals and the Holy Bible."

"And Marmaduke said unto Isaac: Get thee gone and build thee an earthworm, earthwork I would say. And lo it was done and earth did quake with the work thereof."

"I think you laugh at me much of the time."

"Kindly, though. You will admit kindly." They started going down the Steps. "And talking of kindly, would it not be a kindly act to accost the Divine Pauline and speak of her brother, saying he is well and digging hard?"

"He is not well. They say he will be dead this time next year." And then: "Accost. I will keep out of the way of her accosting."

"You will be no accostermonger."

"You laugh at me much of the time."

They had come all the way down the Steps, quieter now than in the daytime, and John led Elton to the Barcaccia, whose water music could, with the evening stilling of the piazza, be clearly heard. "This," John said, "tries to sing me to sleep."

"You really are a poetical sort of fellow. And you have really brought out a book?"

"Alas."

Elton chuckled uneasily. "Will we meet tomorrow?"

"Under the ilexes. I've been searching for a rhyme for ilex. We have a terrible language for rhymes, Isaac Marmaduke. It makes poetical engineering most difficult. Here the people shout in rhyme without reason. Put on your armour, duke, be calmer, duke, cried Marmaduke. We're always being betrayed into comedy. You see how difficult it all is. From the sublime to the ridiculous is but a step."

"That's what Bony said. After the retreat out of Russia."

"He may go down in history as a great theoretician of the arts. Well, Mr Elton sir, under the ilexes let it be." Elton, though in civilian dress, sketched a salute and loped off across the piazza towards the Caffé Greco. John stood a while by Bernini's broken marble boat, listening to the water music. He tried to identify himself with the water, to be the water, to feel the small sick parcel of flesh that was himself liquefy joyfully, joyfully relish its own wetness and singing clarity. He sprang back with a start into nerve and bone to find a hand on his arm. James Clark, his doctor, with a smiling stranger. Clark said:

"Ye should be hame the noo, Master Keats. The nicht air—"

"Is nae halesome. Aye, I ken." The stranger looked puzzled with the very puzzlement of Lieutenant Elton. "I mean no mockery," John said. "Doctor Clark knows that his deliberate use of Scotch inspires confidence. Scotch engineers, Scotch doctors—"

"Scotch reviewers," said the stranger.

"Somehow I knew you understood English."

"This is Mr Keats," Clark said. "This is Signor Giovanni Gulielmi, man of letters and citizen of Rome."

"I know your work," said Gulielmi. "I know your *Endymion* well—"

"Ah, no, not that botched mawkery."

"Also your volume of this year. Would you call that too a botched mockery?"

"Mawkery," John corrected. "A neologism. The critics were always on to me for making up words. A real writer, they seemed to imply, would get all his words from Johnson's

Dictionary. Sorry, I seem to start with a mockery and continue with a rebuke. You speak English excellent well, before God, with a right slight accent of the North. I would I had but a hundredth of that skill in the Tuscan."

"In, in," urged Clark, impelling John by the elbow. "Is Mr Severn already at home?"

"I let my keeper loose for the evening. He has gone to see the sculptures of a certain Mr Ewing."

"William Ewing," Gulielmi said. "He has a certain small talent. His figures are recognisably figures, one may say so much."

"I envy," John panted, climbing the marble stairway to the second floor of Number 26, "any man who can carve marble. To climb it," seeing old Mr Gibson come from the top floor, candle-lighted by his French valet, "is for me, in my present state," having just visited Mr O'Hara up there, "work enough. Your servant, sir."

"Evening, evening," old Mr Gibson growled, passing, candle proceeding.

"Easy, man, easy," said Clark, trying to pull John to a standstill by his coattail. "There's all the time in the world." Then he emended: "I' the worrrruld."

John led his visitors into the parlour. Light was fading. He looked panting for candles. Panting less, he sat with Clark and Gulielmi, their shadow selves sitting huge upon the walls. "Wine," he said.

"Tell me where the wine is," said Gulielmi, getting up. "Ah, I see it, I think."

"Your English is astonishingly good, signore."

"Not astonishingly. My maternal grandfather came from Manchester and was a staunch Stuart man. Disgusted and, indeed, disgraced by the failure of the rebellion of 1745, he exiled himself to Italy. He died recently, very old, in an apartment of the Castello on the lake of Bracciano. He was still brooding on the lost Stuart cause, execrating the puddingy Hanoverians, as he called them. My mother, his daughter, keeps my English alive, as does my work as a translator. Our friend Dr Clark has, I fear, little sympathy for the Pretenders. I, though an Anglo-Italian, am a better Scot than he." He smiled though, pouring the cheap golden Roman table wine, all that John and Severn could afford.

"A question of faith," Clark said. "My family is allied to the Knoxes, meaning the great Knox who preached against Mary our Jezebel mistress. As for the Hanoverians, I'll serve them. As for puddingy, your bonny prince was puddingy enough."

"You then, sir I will say and no longer signore, are of the Romish faith?" And then at once: "Oh, it seems I must spend all this evening in apology, for both stupidity and boorishness. Of course you are of the faith, and Romish is a stupid word. For my part, I belong to nothing. I recognise," looking at Clark, "that it might still my soul in face of we know what if I belonged to something. But it is too late, I think. Severn, if I may speak so without disloyalty, does not in his work *in his work* bear the best witness for the Christian creed. It does not help his art, shall I say. Too gentle-Jesus feathery where the iron groin should show through."

"Art," said Clark, "is no, not everything."

"Religious," Gulielmi said, wine up for sipping. "To be religious is to respond to the numinous. It does not have to be your Mr Severn's gentle Jesus. I have read your poems. You treat Apollo, may I say, as a living numen."

John turned big eyes on him that flashed in the candles. "He is not mocked," he said. "That god is not mocked. That god can punish."

"Punish may be, but no save," Clark said.

"Save, yes, that too," John said fiercely. "I will say that only he can save. This you should know, as he is also the god of healing. It was to that side of him I was first led. I was," he told Gulielmi, "once a small sawbones."

"I had heard that."

"I knew that I was to serve one god, but I had mistaken which of his aspects it was to be. Save, yes, save. What does it profit a man to become a saint in heaven? What does it profit them he leaves behind?

"He can intercede," Gulielmi said, with mock primness, "at the Throne of the Most High."

"Saints do not create goodness, they but exemplify it. As for those called by Apollo, they *make* truth, they *make* beauty. They create, and in creating create also themselves. Let us not talk of the Christian God's part in the everlasting making and remaking of the world."

"Ye're unco excited, man," in deliberate Scotch. "It will dae your stomach nae sort o' guid to be in that state."

"My stomach will do well enough," John said stiffly. "It is not my stomach I have to worry about."

"The trouble with the lungs is past. It is in the stomach, it is the stomach that must be watched."

"Dr Clark," John said firmly, "I took this to be a social visit. In the presence of Signor or Mr Gulielmi this talk of stomachs is to say the least unseemly."

I take to him, thought Gulielmi. He is a little man and no more than a boy, but he comports himself with Apollonian dignity. I take to the large eyes and the quivering nose and the big overlip, the strong chin, the hair that is both fire and cornfield. Can he live to be a poet? He cannot breathe well, but he looks well supplied of energy. He said: "I will be happy to hear of stomachs in a capacity not clinical. Are you eating well here in Rome?"

"Now well," John said. "Filthily before. But I threw our imported dinner out of that window two afternoons ago. Scrawny raw chicken and filthy macaroni and filthier rice pudding out on to the steps for the dogs to pounce on. So the point was well taken and the trattoria now sends up food we can eat. The action was better than any speech. It was done with a smile and the fellow with the basket smiled too."

"And your Italian, how is your Italian?"

"I read Dante with the help of Cary's translation. Reading is, however, not speaking."

"You must learn our Roman speech, it may amuse you."

"There's hardly time." It was said without self-pity. They heard boots on marble approaching. "Severn," said John. "Sabrina fair." The young man who entered, mouth open smilingly as to drink in cheerfully whatever the evening sent by way of company, was indeed fair though somewhat washed out, his good looks girlish enough. He was introduced to Gulielmi. He said, with an atrocious accent:

"Parla bene il signore la nostra lingua."

John said: "It's his mother's—Italojacobite exilic, Charlie is my darling. How were the Ewing marbles?"

"I think," said Severn reverently, "he has an exquisite talent. There is a quality of true sentiment, the stone eyes have a look positively languishing in one of his demure maidens. He has done a pair of spaniels that belie their marble. His marble comes from Pietrasanta, where Michelangelo got his. That alone makes him take fire. Oh yes, exquisite work."

"Alas alas," Gulielmi said, "it was not the marble that Michelangelo would have chosen if he had had any say in the matter. His and everyone's preferred blocks come from Carrara. But he was at work on Medici commissions and the Medici family owned the Pietrasanta quarries and imposed their stuff upon him. Soft and dirty he called it." The poet's eyes smiled. I take to him, thought Gulielmi.

"Ewing in Italy," John said, "hewing so prettily."

"Oh, very prettily, John," Severn said. "You must come, you will be impressed."

"I must be impressed to come, press-ganged. I have had my fill of marble and only half-digested it. The Elgins, I chew their cud still. Give us some music, Severn. Something not too melting."

All this time, nursing his rebuke, Clark had said nothing. Now he said: "Haydn."

John smiled and said: "We are grateful, Dr Clark, you must know that. For the loan of your music. For much else." Clark reluctantly smiled back.

Severn pulled at his fingers, cracking them, then sat at the ill-tuned pianoforte they had rented. He played the first movement of a Haydn sonata, one in D major. John leaned on the instrument, surveying Severn's dancing or walking fingers in wonder. "He's like a child," he said in glee at the end. "You never know what he will do next."

Severn looked faintly offended. "I can assure you, John, I followed the notes as written."

"I meant Haydn, not you. And yet we *do* know what he will do next. I dedicate this evening to the bubbling out of stupidities. Play that movement again and I will know what he is going to do next. If I could read those hieroglyphics I would see it all planned, not at all childlike." In comic gloom, "It justifies or vindicates or something Dr Clark's John Calvin. All planned from start to end and I am fool enough to talk of childish unpredictability." He chuckled. "Still, it is a good impersonation of child-likeness. Not like old Willy Wordsworth."

Severn did not attack the second movement. He folded his hands and looked up in reproach. "These days you laugh at everything."

"Not at everything, Sabrina. I do not laugh at our comic writers."

"I think," Gulielmi said, "you must plunge into our Roman dialect at once. It is not like the Tuscan. Its very make and sound is different. And it has never had the terrible dantesco vision imposed on it. It does not have that sense of high responsibility that for half a millennium the tongue of Florence has had to bear. The Roman tongue is coarse and rough and full of the Rabelaisian. There are, for instance, hundreds of words to describe, to describe, well, the—"

"Ah," John said, "I see we are on the marge of bawdry. Can you *stomach* some of that commodity, Dr Clark? Severn can drown his ears in Haydn."

"I have a friend," Gulielmi said, "a poet, scholar, actor, a fine-looking man, a fine man altogether, who did an admirable thing and then, in a sort of pudic remorse, destroyed it. His copy, that is. I had and have my own. A sonnet based on the Roman cant terms for the ah male pudendum. A long sonnet."

"I do not think, with respect," John said, "you may speak of a long sonnet."

"Come, you will have met sonnets with codas. Petrarch wrote them. Your, our, Milton wrote one too."

"I'm stupid again. Of course. A sonnet on the penis with a tail. Just, very just. Who is your friend?"

"A man tugged many ways—towards respectability, even holiness, towards the dirty suffering life of the holy and unholy city the papal rule has made, on its surface, somewhat dull and conforming. You see, sir, we may love our popes spiritually but, in the secular sphere, be unhappy about them. However. If you want laughter here, you will find it in the obscenity of desperation."

"That," John said, his face glowing in the pianoforte candles, "is a fine phrase, obscenity of desperation is a."

"I will give you a fine word," Gulielmi said, "that you will not find in Dante. It is for the male organ and it is *dumpennente*. Is not that a fine word?"

"I think," Dr Clark said, in unscotch, "Mr Keats has had enough excitement for the evening. I would say it is time for him to go to his bed."

"Taking with him his lonely *dumpennente*," John said. He kissed the delicious word. "*Duuuuuum*—A pendent pen, dumb and in the dumps."

"Yes, you see the way Roman language operates. An n and a d following become a double n. *Dumpendente*. The origin of course is the Latin *dum pendebat*. You catch the reference? No?

Stabat mater dolorosa
Apud lignum lachrymosa
Dum pendebat filius."

"An unholy reference, if I may say so," Severn said, unwontedly assertive, the Haydn slow movement evidently not now to be attacked.

"Come, Mr Severn, I take you to be of the Reformed Faith. It is our *Stabat Mater,* not yours, and we may do blasphemies with it if we will."

"Blasphemy is blasphemy."

"One and indivisible," said John with joy. "Severn gets his *Stabat Mater* from Haydn or Mozart or somebody. But how wonderful—*dum pendebat*—while he was hanging. From the cross, from the crotch. But this is exquisite, and in no feathery way. This is the good groiny iron. You've given me a fine present, Mr Gulielmi."

"There are more in store, if you will have them."

"We will go," Dr Clark said sternly. He returned to Scotch, language of health and holiness, for his patient. "Ye're unco excitable, ye ken that? Bye and bye I maun consider what tae dae wi' yon stomach."

John facetiously took the yon for a true yonder and peered for the stomach in the corner shadows. "Aye," he then smiled. "Bye and bye is easily said. I do not mock. Remember I am still, on engrossed and wax-sigillaed parchment, of your confraternity. I do not think it is the stomach."

"We will see."

"Alas, yes. *You* will see."

When the visitors had left, Severn and John looked at each other. Severn brought the pianoforte lid gently down and looked again. John's eyes were now dulled, stilled, the lids brought gently down. He was sitting with left foot on right knee, shoe off, fondling his instep. He said:

"You were shocked. You will be shocked more before we are done."

"It is not to my taste, no more than that. It will seem namby pamby to you that I spoke so, but it is the way I was brought up. You are unused to Christians, I know. I think sometimes now of Providence. My being here, I mean."

"Cant and humbug, by your leave. Anyway, I talk of bigger shocks. The obscenity not of desperation but of dying. It will not be pretty, like some marble spaniel of Mr Ewing. Are you sure you wish to stay?"

"If I did not love you I would still speak of my Christian duty. Besides, I do not believe it. You are already better."

"In terms of my posthumous life, yes. I am not spewing blood. I fear our friend Clark may be right. I have pains in my stomach. I may add I have pain in my dumpendebat. Oh no, don't look newly shocked, nothing to do with the clap, big or little. Shall I say that I have loved like a gentleman, meaning to end unfulfilled, not to have cupped those breasts naked or even kissed deeply, and as for the other, the right true end—And I am wrong too to say *gentleman*, because we have been confined by our class which is neither gentlemanly nor ruffianly but plain pure middle, and poets of the middle zone are not permitted, by reason of their small sales, to be married. So I end unsatisfied, Severn my dear boy, and I would curse loudly now if I were not so, ah, spent. Spent without spending."

"But you have— You told me. I mean, the experience, though not with."

"I've drabbed, briefly and cheaply. That I try to forget."

"You really mean," Severn said, with the eye of fascination

all against his better instincts, "you think she should have— given herself to you?"

"Like you, like Lieutenant Isaac Marmaduke Elton, she accepts the cant of the feathers and the iron meeting holily when the holy words have been burbled. Poets do not marry, though. Not on a sale of fifty copies."

Severn, still standing by the pianoforte, lifted the limp wings of his arms to waist height then let them limply fall. "Lord Byron can live on his verse. But who would wish to be Lord Byron?" A candle flickered at that question, and a wind brought the chuckle of the fountain a fraction nearer. "It is love that is the thing, remember, the warmth of two hearts conjoined. She returns your love."

"*Dum pendebat* on the *crux* she returned his *amore*. And yet her name, now I say it to myself in this room, Rome I would say where names are tunes—" He was weary. "The name of any leering fishwife. A seller of headcheese. Give me some of my laudanum, Severn. I need sleep."

"I gave it to Dr Clark, you know that. I want no repetition of what of what."

"Happened on the ship to Naples. Good. The suicidal poet must be protected from himself. Good good. Meanwhile I may not sleep."

"The fountain will send you off. You say it does."

"By the waters of babble on there we shat down and flung our arses on the pillows."

"That is not funny."

"No, merely blasphemous. I blaspheme against love and against both testicles I would say testaments. But a testimony is to do with swearing on one's balls. An old Roman custom. And there are *two* testaments. Interesting."

"If blaspheming makes you more cheerful, then I suppose you must blaspheme," Severn said stoically. "But I wish there were some other way of making you cheerful."

Soon John lay in the Roman dark listening to the fountain he thought of as his. It was not a question of being cheerful, rather of shedding the shameful rotting stuff that was himself by making that inner nub which cried I, I, I into the centre of something free of the agony of thought. He tried to turn himself into the music of Haydn that Severn had played, but the image of Severn's all too human fingers intruded like a meddling elf. As for the water of the fountain, it remained obdurately other, singing mindlessly and unoppressed by time.

II

GIOVANNI GULIELMI, DOCTOR OF LETTERS OF THE University of Bologna, had a small private income, derived from the rents of the land in Lazio left him by his father, who was untimely dead of Naples cholera, some British gold invested with the banker Torlonia, and what he got from the tenants of the first and second floors of the large house facing the Basilica of Santa Cecilia in the piazza named for her in the Trastevere district of Rome. The third, top, floor was enough for his mother and himself. Their cook and maid lived out. They had no coach. Gulielmi had a study of his own, very bare, with rugs on the marble, a massive English mahogany table that had been his maternal grandfather's, and three pictures on the walls. These were respectively by Labella, Macellari and Zappone, minor painters of respectively the Umbrian, Florentine and Venetian schools, and were respectively of the Annunciation, the Jordan Baptism and the Scourging at the Pillar. Here he worked at translations from English into Tuscan—unprofitable work, except for his version of Byron's *Beppo,* which had gone into three Turin printings. He sat with *Endymion* and the 1820 poems of John Keats and the fine-eyed, wavy-maned Giuseppe Gioacchino Belli one forenoon of November sunlight and intense blue Roman sky, song and the noise of fish and vegetable vendors coming from below. Belli looked without favour at the beginning of Gulielmi's draft translation of the *Ode to a Nightingale.*

"'My heart is sad and my senses are oppressed by a stupor as of sleep, as if I had been drinking hemlock.' Yes yes

yes. What does he know about drinking hemlock? We have all heard this kind of thing before."

"The content, yes. The shape, the melody, no."

"Which you cannot translate."

"That argues its superiority as poetry. Byron is all too translatable."

"Poetry should be *about* things. What things is poetry about since 1815? The poet's mistress is cruel to him. The poet fears he is going to die or fears he is not going to die. Rather like seasickness. The world is a fearful emptiness, but birds and flowers grant some little consolation. Perhaps next year there will be a new subject, but I think most poets have their elegies on Napoleon waiting."

"Here is something different," Gulielmi said, picking up a single sheet from his table. "The young man gave me this as an example of a sonnet in the Petrarchan form, difficult in a language like English, which has so few rhymes."

"Why does it have few rhymes? It is not natural for a language to have few rhymes. Italian is full of rhymes."

"Something to do with the endings dropping off," Gulielmi vaguely said.

"I cannot understand English and you say this little man is untranslatable."

"This poem is about a cat. A cat belonging to some lady called Signora Reynolds."

"Facetious then, light, nothing."

"Catullus wrote on a sparrow."

"Light, nothing."

"But listen to the sound. It sounds like a cat."

"A *sonnet?*"

"Listen.

'Cat, who hast past thy Grand Climacteric,
How many mice and rats hast in thy days
Destroy'd? – how many tit bits stolen? Gaze
With those bright languid segments green and prick
Those velvet ears—but pr'ythee do not stick
Thy latent talons in me—' "

"Enough. It is nothing but noise."

"*Latent* applied to claws is good. *Latentes.* What to an Englishman is an abstract Latin word takes on here the right physical attributes. The claws are not just hidden but *latent*— ready to come out. Not just hidden but known to be hidden. Like Christ in the tabernacle."

"Blasphemy blasphemy blasph—"

"Blasphemy to discuss the word *latens?*"

"It is a bad poem."

"But you don't quite understand my meaning, his—"

"Nor do I wish to."

"Let me finish. It's only fourteen lines."

Belli got up from his chair, really a kind of Scotch creepy-stool, and addressed an invisible audience of academicians. "Gentlemen," he declaimed, "I have an astonishing new discovery to impart. The sonnet-form is at last known to possess fourteen lines. The truth has been ascertained and confirmed beyond all possible shade of doubt by means of the new computorial digital device invented by the learned and honourable Doctor Giovanni Gulielmi—"

"Let me finish," said Gulielmi, grinning, "damn you."

"As the man said to the whore who received a message her mother was dying. No, no, I am sorry. That was unworthy. There is something unworthy in me that spurts out, like a night emission. There I go again. I am sorry, sorry. This lowness in myself. I try to subdue it." He beat his breast thrice and histrionically. And then: "It's a strong hand," he admitted, glancing at the manuscript before, with heavy grace, reseating himself. "More of a man's hand than a boy's."

"He's only a few years younger than you, than me."

"He has a boy's mind. Finish the thing."

> " '—and upraise
> Thy gentle mew – and tell me all thy frays
> Of Fish and Mice, and Rats and tender chick.' "

"So ends the octave," Belli said. "I can tell it was the octave. But what noises—*eis, icch.*"

"Cat noises. Listen.

> 'Nay look not down, nor lick thy dainty wrists—
> For all the wheezy Asthma—and for all
> Thy tail's tip is nicked off—and though the fists
> Of many a maid have given thee many a maul,
> Still is that fur as soft as when the lists
> In youth thou enter'dst on glass-bottled wall.' "

Belli made a cabbage of his face, as though, for a large audience, enacting nausea. "Such noises. *Th* and *tch* and *rdst* and *glsbtld.* English has no music."

"May it not be that Italian has too much music?"

Belli thought about that. "Write a sonnet in Tuscan about a cat," he then said, "not that any poet should or would, and you would have the creature presented through a lithe and sinuous melody of exquisite verbal configurations."

"This is an old battle-scarred cat, its ears nicked, full of asthma. It is no feline odalisque. Try those last two lines in Italian and see what you get. Let's see. *'Pur'ora morbido é il manto tuo come ai di' delle lizze che giostravi tra cocci di bottiglie a co' di molti muri di cinta.'*"

"That's not poetry."

"Nor is it cats fighting on a wall. Poetry or not, it's still too musical. Our language is full of damnable chiming bells."

"On cue." Belli grinned as the Angelus started. "You timed that well, you had your eye on your watch." He went over to the window and opened it to let the bell-clash swagger in. He leaned on the sill to look down on buying and selling Trasteverines. "Look down on our buying and selling Trasteverines," he said. "How do they think of the Angelic Annunciation, if they think of it at all? A girl called Maria slurping her noonday minestra, probably with the Angelus clanging outside, the angel whizzing in like a wasp through a broken window to tell her that a bird has laid an egg in her belly. How would your Misiter Kettis like that, the respectable cat-loving Englishman?"

"The joke could not be conveyed in English. The English do not call a penis a bird."

Belli turned his back on the sky and bells and harlequin-pied street-scene with actor's swiftness. "There I go again. I must attend to what I say. I am not serious enough. God forgive me." It was a little too much like acting, Gulielmi thought, and not good acting. Belli had been merely an amateur actor. Also amateur billiards-player, amateur poet. In what then was he professional? Minor officer in the Stamp Department of the Government of the Holy City? He would not admit where his professionalism lay or could lie, would he but cease to resist its pull. It lay precisely in the image of a slattern called Mary slurping her soup and the Archangel Gabriel buzzing in like a wasp, in the conveying of that image in the soiled language of the streets. It lay in a perhaps never to be written sonnet on a Roman cat, mauled, torn and randy, ready to piss on any cardinal's robe that offered. Something better than Keats could ever do. Gulielmi said:

"For God's sake, what do you mean by *serious?*"

"Eternal truths," Belli said too promptly, "impressive spiritual essences, God and country and the roaring giants of history. Not, by Bacchus, cats."

"Cats are the eternal truths, and the taste of noonday soup, and farting, and snot, and the itch on your back you can't quite reach to scratch. Rome as those lying and cheating bastards down there, not Rome as the imperial or the papal *essence.* Think of all those odes to Bonaparte, where are they now? The reality, and you can read of it in the *Gazette de Francfort,* is a swollen body on St Helena and the cancers working away in it."

Belli bunched his fine face, shrugged, belched out a Roman *beeeeeeh,* became upright and handsome and *serious.* "A balance should be possible. Between the claims of the physically transient and the spiritually permanent. But finally it is the spirit that counts, since, as you say, there is a dying body on St Helena. Poetry should hymn the spirit and not talk of asthmatic cats."

"We've had too much spirit, I think. I think the time is coming when sonnets must be written about the pains of constipation."

"You go too far as ever, but I forgive you. I am due back now at the office. When shall we eat supper somewhere?"

"I think we ought to eat supper with this young poet. He is altogether *aimable,* totally *simpatico.* You will like him."

"I speak no English. He speaks no Italian."

"A little. He's reading Italian. He has a volume of Alfieri."

"That will make him very gloomy."

"He also has some French. Less than you, true, but some."

Gulielmi did not say that John Keats also had a fair copy of a rejected sonnet-with-coda written by Belli, a regretted dirty joke, the something regrettable that got into him and out again. He said instead:

"We could give him supper in some osteria. This Scotch doctor is starving him for his stomach's sake."

"Let him read his Alfieri and learn serious Italian. Then perhaps we can talk seriously about the great tragic themes and the difficult art of rhetoric. But cats' claws, no. Fighting on walls and getting nicked ears, no. Shameful triviality." The bells clashed on.

III

THE BELLS CLASHED ON JOHN KEATS TRYING TO STILL THE
anguish in himself by looking out of the casement on to the
noonday magic of the piazza. Flower-carts blazed, their hues
somehow sharpened by the bell harmonics seething from the
Church of the Trinitá dei Monti. Artist's models, men, women,
children, lounged in easy grace on the steps, waiting for or rest-
ing from employment in this piazza of painters, clad in the bright
raw costumes of the regions of Italy. Trying to still the anguish
that had come upon him on the very second page of the volume
of Alfieri. Such words did not help his condition: "Unhappy me!
No solace remains but weeping, and weeping is a crime." No
more Alfieri. Tasso? To go back to Tasso, poet of his boyhood,
though now in the original sunlit language that foggy English
blurred, would but be to be reminded that the ambition to be
as great as Tasso could never now be fulfilled. He felt two slow
tears, criminal, sluggishly coursing but wiped them soon. Were
Severn here he would be over-sympathetic and try to insinuate
in some trite Jesus consolation, but Severn was working at what
he called his art in his room. So John now took from its hid-
ingplace within the pages of Tasso the manuscript sonnet (with
coda) that Gulielmi, along with a literal translation, had given
him. The poet's name was not to be disclosed, for the poet had
abandoned his poem in hot shame, breast-beating.

The poem was in the Roman dialect, not easy to understand,
but two known words leered out—*cazzo* and that glorious
dumpendenne—like a whore's eyes from an alley, bringing to

his own *cazzo* or dumpendebat that quickening he had always associated with the creative itch. The poem was but an obscene catalogue, a rhymed dirty glossary, ennobled (stiffened?) by the stringency of its form. But why not? He went to the table, found foolscap under the book-pile, sharpened a quill, dipped in the ferrous ink, began to paraphrase:

> Here are some names, my son, we call the prick:
>> The chair, the yard, the nail, the kit, the cock,
>> The holofernes, rod, the sugar rock,
> The dickory dickory dock, the liquorice stick,
> The lusty Richard or the listless Dick,
>> The old blind man, the jump on twelve o'clock,
>> Mercurial finger, or the lead-fill'd sock,
> The monkey, or the mule with latent kick.

He smiled at himself, finishing the octave—John Keats, lush or mawkish quite-the-little-poet. What would the *Edinburgh Review* say of this? Would Leigh Hunt print it in the *Examiner* and go to jail again on behalf of Free Speech? This will never do. He took breath and dove at the sestet:

> The squib, the rocket, or the roman candle,
>> The dumpendebat or the shagging shad,
> The love-lump or the hump or the pump-handle,
>> The tap of venery, the leering lad,
> The handy dandy, stiff-proud or a-dandle,
>> But most of all our Sad Glad Bad Mad Dad.

And what to do with this—send it to brother George and sister-in-law Georgiana to read, breath of home, under the sumacs or sequoias, savage Indians who had not read Rousseau whooping warlike all around? Read it to Severn and have him run off screaming to pack his bags? The coda now, just like Milton in his *Late Enforcers of Conscience* if that was the right title.

> And I might add
>> That learned pedants burning midnight tapers
>> Find Phallus, apt for their scholastic papers,
>> And one old man I know calls it Priapus.
> His wife has no word for it but a sigh—
> A sign that Joy has somehow past her by.

Or would "failed to satisfy" be better? Change "Joy" to "Life"? No matter. Well, could there be purer art than this well-wrought urn of elegant impurities? It was for no audience. Art at the last was between the artist and his god.

The ink dried, no need for sanding, while he read it through again. So his last poem would be no more than an obscenity, though might not obscenity be another name for homage to those primal and universal urges that Society & Religion, as Shelley had said once at Hunt's, clok'd through Fear? A primal urge denied all but those who could drab without shame or remorse, taking their salvatory mercury after as he had once done, following that night at Oxford best forgotten. For there had to be Love. He was ready to weep again, and then his self-pity was transformed to anger. But there on the table was his *Anatomy of Melancholy,* which was full of as it were comfortably tooth-sucking-after-dinner injunctions to season all with laughter. If Robert Burton were here he might read this tailed sonnet with gusto.

After dinner John went for his walk on the Pincio and found Isaac Marmaduke Elton already there under the ilexes, looking out towards the grape-hued cupola of St Peter's in the citron light. John tapped his left breast where the sonnet nested, smiled to himself, wondered whether this soldier might—

"I have a thing here," he said, "which may amuse you." But Elton, whose straight back he had addressed, turned stiffly in what John divined was a posture of distress and passed a fist rapidly over his eyes. "What is the matter? Some bad news—" The death-sentence for this soldier who had thought his lungs to be improving? Elton sighed and made a shrugging gesture he had, probably not by intention, picked up here in Rome. He said:

"Tomorrow I go to Naples, thence to sail to England. They say I am better. Much better," he repeated in bitterness.

"I am glad, though selfishly sorry as well. I shall miss our walks and talks. You don't seem very happy at being much better."

"This," Elton said, and he thrust a paper at John with a straight arm as in a drill movement. "There is still light enough for you to read. And there is not much to read."

"Her name is what? I take it to be *her*—I cannot quite— The signature is all cramped together."

"Augusta. Her name is Augusta. Not that it matters."

Augusta was Georgiana's other name. The letter, though, was not of the kind that Georgiana could ever write, not an intrepid girl daring the same fevers and arrows as her husband John's brother in America's wilderness. This was a spoiled young miss. "Dearest Marmaduke, you will recall how you gave me leave to regard myself as free from the obligations of our betrothal & how I said no I will wait for ever if need be.

Mama has talked much of this & much prais'd your goodness & braveness & magnanimity—" Silly girl, silly uneducated miss. And so, John distractedly noticed, he was a Marmaduke after all. Probably Marmadukes received letters like this more often than Isaacs. "—I cried much but see how she is right that I am the eldest & have obligations to her & to papa & to Jane & Emma & Lizzy. So I accept that our engagement is at an end & now I am engag'd to be married to—" Some soldier or other, a fellow officer of dearest Marmaduke.

"I'm sorry," John said. The letter ended with something about loving dearest Marmaduke eternally like a brother and perhaps everything would be put right in heaven. Ever your loving.

"Accursed, accursed, they cannot be trusted, not one of them. And to think it should be *him*. And to receive that *now*—"

"The thing to do is not to let this set you back. You owe it to your health not to— I mean, to fall into a melancholy is the very worst thing—"

"I gave her everything—my heart, I promised chastity despite all a soldier's soldier's—"

"Temptations, yes, I see. We had best go to some wineshop and—"

"Drink, yes, drab, yes, for they are all nothing, they are things to be used and then flung away. I gave her everything, I gave her all my love—"

Pauline Bonaparte glided through the twilight, two servants keeping their distance behind. She was exquisite in taffetas. She turned her great eyes frankly, as before, on Elton. Elton spoke. Elton said:

"*Madame, vous ne me verrez plus. Je m'en irai demain.*

J'ai été blessé, oui, mortellement blessé par une femme. Malédictions à votre sexe, madame, un sexe tout à fait maudit, madame—"

Pauline Bonaparte seemed no whit put out, maledictions on her sex being truly tributes to the power of it. But John cut into Elton's bad French with his own mongrel Romance:

"Altessa, cara principessa, mon ami est souffrant, la sua inamorata non, ne, sa fiancée, vous comprenez, aime un altro. Her love is dead."

"It is my love that is dead, damn her."

Pauline Bonaparte, to John's surprise but Elton's incomprehension, spoke Latin: *"Alma Venus, caeli subter labentia signa quae mare navigerum, quae terras frugiferentes concelebras—"* Then she waved the citation away into the twilight with a graceful snaking of her arm. She said: "Lucrezio." Then, smiling brilliantly, she swayed off, servants keeping their distance after.

"What was all that about?" said Elton. "Who's this Lucrezio?"

"Lucretius," John said. "Strange, I'd never have believed she knew Latin. That was the opening invocation to Venus in *De Rerum Natura*. What she was saying was that love doesn't die, not in the bigger sense. Everything grovels to Venus. She'll have you yet, Isaac Marmaduke."

"I'm leaving tomorrow, I told you I was leaving."

"Yes, yes, but she'll have you yet. *Alma Venus* won't leave you alone for long."

They went down the Steps in silence for a while. Then John said: "I see it, of course, I see the whole picture. Quite a little poem. The divine Pauline reclines as Venus reclining for Canova, and Canova gives her those lines to learn and repeat

over and over, stop her fidgeting. That accent, I should suppose, is Corsican."

"Damn her, damn all of them, bitches."

They turned into a side-street off the piazza and went into
a tavern. There were smoky oil-lamps and a few other drink-
ers, big-shouldered sincerely voluble Romans who stared their
fill, moving their big bulks bodily the better to stare, and then
resumed vivid gesture-sauced colloquies. A crone who limped
brought wine.

"You know what it looks like?" Elton said. "It looks like
horse-piss."

"It tastes well enough. A little acidulous. Strange how things
always read better than they taste. Acorns and cheese brick-
hard in *Don Quixote,* the wineskin cooling in the leaves—no
meal more delicious in print. Wine in poetry is superior to wine
in a glass. What will you do?"

"When I go back? I don't know what I will do. I loved her,
you see." He had the sort of classical beauty that became inhu-
man when attacked by grief, a Greek façade meant only for
sunlight. Gothic was best, John thought, looking at the face
prepared to crumble into snivels, Gothic was built for storms.
He said quickly:

"You should read Burton. Listen." And he began to recite
the one paragraph of the *Anatomy of Melancholy* he had com-
mitted to memory. "'Love is blind, as the saying is, Cupid's
blind, and so are all his followers. Every lover admires his mistress, though she be very deformed of herself, ill-favoured,
wrinkled, pimpled, pale, red, yellow, tanned, tallow-faced, have
a swollen juggler's platter face, or a thin lean chitty face,
have clouds in her eyes, be crooked, dry bald, goggle-eyed,
blear-eyed, or with staring eyes, she looks like a squised cat,

hold her head still awry, heavy, dull, hollow-eyed, black or yellow about the eyes, or squint-eyed, sparrow-mouthed, Persian hook-nosed, have a sharp fox-nose, a red nose, China flat, great nose, snub and flat nose, a nose like a promontory, gubbertushed, rotten teeth, black, uneven, brown teeth, beetle-browed, a witch's beard, her breath stink all over the room, her nose drop winter and summer, with a Bavarian poke under her chin, a sharp chin, lave-eared, with a long crane's neck which stands awry too, her dugs like two double jugs, or else no dugs, bloody-fallen fingers, she have long filthy unpared nails, scabbed hands or wrists, a tanned skin, a rotten carcass, crooked back, she stoops, is lame, splay-footed, as slender in the middle as a cow in the waist, gouty legs, her ankles hang over her shoes, her feet stink, she breed lice, a mere changeling, a very monster, an oaf imperfect, her whole complexion savours, an harsh voice, incondite gesture, vile gait, a vast virago, or an ugly tit, a slug, a fat fustilugs, a truss, a long lean rawbone, a skeleton, and to thy judgment looks like a mard in a lanthorn, whom thou couldst not fancy for a world, but hatest, loathest, and wouldst have spit in her face, or blow thy nose in her bosom, *remedium amoris* to another man, a dowdy, a slut, a scold, a nasty rank rammy filthy beastly quean, dishonest peradventure, obscene, base, beggarly, rude, foolish, untaught, peevish—if he love her once, he admires her for all this, he takes no notice of any such errors or imperfections of body or mind, he had rather have her than any woman in the world.' "

Even the Romans had been listening from about half-way through the catalogue, openmouthed. One old man said *"Bravo"* at the end. Elton goggled at Keats, his face restored to handsomeness, very vacuous.

"Why?" he said: "Why did you learn all that?"

"I like it," John said. "Besides, it's a manner of warning. Not to fall in love."

"But the whole drift is, as I see it, that love is strong and mighty and overcomes reason."

"Yes yes, I see, I know. Shakespeare was shorter with his brow of Egypt. *Alma Venus* works through madness." He drank. The wine took fire from the lantern on its shelf on the roughcast wall beside them. "Sour. I used Burton's book once to a very practical end. I used advice he gives for the stemming of lust. It was difficult for me at that time, you see. I was sharing a house with a man, and he was sharing his bed with the Irish maidservant. I could hear them every night and sometimes in the afternoon. And there was I in love, and desirous, and not able— Burton advised the thinning out of the diet. I took no meat, no wine. I was a very Hindoo with my mess of greens. It subdued desire and I was able to concentrate on love. What kind of a world is it that denies the goddess to us? *Alma Venus,* indeed, ruling all. She does not rule the way we of the middle sort must love."

Elton's face began unbecomingly to crack again. "It is not just any body, not just any breasts or buttocks or— It is hers under the muslin. Hers, hers only. Now Major Kettering will thrust in."

"Is this the Harry she speaks of?"

"I know him, I know the swine. We were at Rochester together. God curse, God damn—"

"For God's sake think of it as mere madness. Something that must be cured."

"Are *you* cured?"

John thought about that. "Perhaps," he said at length, "if you ate a beefsteak."

"Here? Beefsteaks here in this town? It's all veal. Their calves never reach bullockhood."

"That's good, that's well put. Here, read this. It is a translation I have done from the holy Roman." And he drew the tailed sonnet from his bosom and handed it to Elton. Elton read it with gloom as though it were a move-order back to St Helena.

"Coarse. I know all of these words for the member save that one—*dumpendebat*. That you made up."

"It's a holy word from a holy hymn."

"Major Kettering with his holy dumpendebat, thrusting it in. There were some of us after supper, pissing in the garden of the mess at Rochester, with the orchestra coming through very clear and the swish of the dancers, for it was our summer ball. Pissing under the stars and on the bole of the great elm that's there. One said, Captain Freebody I believe it was, there's an unholy great red rod you have on you, Harry. And Kettering says: made great with use. It all comes back to me now. God, God, surely that's where they met. And Augusta so demure in her spotted muslin ballgown, and her arms so tender and plump." Elton began to cry.

"Stop that," John said sharply. "We all have cause for it. It's not a man's way."

"Man's way." Elton stiffened. "Damn you, I'm a soldier," he cried, then drank off his wine, shuddered, poured himself all that was left in the fiasco and, before drinking again, called: "Hey grandma, more of this piss." The Romans heard that— *thispis*—with the respect due to an older and more authoritative tongue than their own, perhaps Greek, and tried it out *(dispis)* while the old woman, with a gummy garlic cackle, went to refill. "How did you get yours?" Elton asked.

"My what?"

"The thing we both have."

"I was nursing my brother," John said. "Tom. A mere boy. I caught it from him."

"And how did he catch it?"

"I don't know. But it can be a very catching thing, God help us."

"But not everybody catches it. The doctors don't seem to catch it. You know what I was told? I was told that all depends on the state of health of the mind of him who is exposed to it. And that if you are in love—if you are thwarted—"

"Please. Try not to think of it." The wine came. "*Grazie.*"

"I put this as a general proposition, you understand, a general proposition." He took comfort from the words and quaffed like a soldier. "What was I saying then?"

"You were, sir, enunciating a general proposition."

"Good. The thwarting of desire, I said. His desire was thwarted. Yours also. And of course mine." He lowered his forehead almost as far as his wine-gripping hand and growled: "Desire."

"You speak better than you know," John said. "There was a fool, his name was Wells, not that it matters. No, it does. Wells of stupidity, of malice, wells of the rank stinking water of inhumanity. He convinced poor Tom that a foreign lady was madly in love with him. She did not, I may say, exist. But Tom in his fever cried out for her. I should have thrashed Wells before I left England."

"I had a corporal named Wells. He was a corrupt man and a drinker. No, his name was Willis. But it is near enough. I'll thrash this Wells for you when I reach home." Erect again, he nodded at John casually, as though he had offered to deliver a parcel. Then: "I have a confession to make."

"Make no confession to me. There's that chewing nodding priest at Trinity Church we see on the Steps. He hears confessions."

"Now you joke again and laugh at me. No, no, this is a confession that concerns only you. I lied to you, you see. I was never at St Helena. It was my cousin Jenkins that was there."

"You were very convincing."

"A lie, yes. But you lie, do you not? Is it not all lying with you? Is not your poetry a kind of lying?"

"A very Platonic way of looking at it. Fictions, yes, the making up of things, but with no intent to deceive. Coleridge says something about the willing suspension of disbelief. Your lie was charming and harmed no one. It was a kind of poetry. That was good, I thought, old Bony shouting Voltaire at you from his cabbage patch."

"Yes, I thought so too. It *could* have happened, could it not? I *could* have been posted to St Helena. In the army you are liable to be posted *anywhere*."

"Where were you in fact posted? When, according to your fiction, you were posted to St Helena."

"Oh, I was in Chatham. And now, naturally, you are fully within your rights not to believe that either."

"I believe. *Credo*. I believe any man who tells me he was at Chatham."

"Well, we must drink to it, we must sink a bumper."

"With all my heart."

Elton looked at John with a cunning kind of frowning. "You do not take me in, you know. You pretend things, but you are laughing at me all the while."

"I assure you I am not."

"To what is it that I just now proposed we drink then?"

"To Chatham, to St Helena, to the mendacious arts, to your recovery. We have forgotten your good news. You're no longer a sick man."

"Oh, I am very sick." Elton bitterly bit off the word several times to the interest of the Romans. "Seck," one of them ventured. "Aye, sick," cried Elton. "What do you common labouring louts know of the soul's sickness? I have given her everything and now she raises her petticoat for the pleasure of Major Kettering. He will pleasure her, aye." A gnarled wall-eyed huge-shouldered Roman nodded with Elton, also saying *ai*. "I will not have your mockery," Elton cried, "I have been mocked enough." He started to rise. John tried to hold him down, saying:

"No, man, sit. This wine is stronger than you think. Do not let the wine talk for you."

"My sword shall talk for me, damn you."

"You're wearing no sword."

"Am I not?" Elton, in surprise that seemed to contain no displeasure, tapped his swordside and looked down on it, then sat. "I must have forgotten to put it on," he said, smiling.

"But you're not in uniform, are you? You are dressed as I am."

"I am better dressed than you are, sir." Elton sped to becoming haughty and truculent drunk.

"You are a gentleman, sir, an officer, sir, and I am but a poor poet, sir."

"And a liar, sir, remember that, sir."

"It is you who are the liar, sir, and on your own admission, sir."

Elton drunk-thundered: "No man calls me a liar, sir." And then he sillily smiled. "Let us have all that again, about foul fustilugs and she is like a cow in the waist and her feet stink and so on." And then, in fine truculence, "It is a foul libel on the sex, sir."

"All of it?"

Elton simpered. "Some of it. What was all that about gubber-somethinged and a sharp fox-nose?"

"I am too weary to do it all again."

"It is true, though," pouted Elton, his eyes stern. "The nose, I mean. I had always wondered what her nose reminded me of, and it was of a fox's. Vixen's, rather. A very small vixen, though, and her nose was always very cold. A sign of health, they say." He felt his own nose. "A sign of good health, so they have always said." He started to laugh. "Blow thy nose in her bosom," he laughed. "The old rogue, whoever he was."

"You are emerging from the dark wood of sadness."

"Oh, but I'm sick, very sick. I love you, madam, but I have taken a severe cold. Permit me to blow my nose in your bosom." He laughed hard and then began to cough. He looked alarmed, coughing and not able to stop. John clapped his back, soft, hard, harder. Elton choked. He searched for his handkerchief and found it at last in his left sleeve. He spat heavily into it. He peered in the lamplight at the gob and said, "Oh no." He moaned.

"It may be the wine," John said, his heart stirred to pity and referred fear. But of course the wine was white, urine.

Elton sternly stowed the wrapped sputum in his right sleeve. "Tell no one," he ordered. "Don't tell that fool Clark."

"You must see Clark. At once."

"What will he do, the fool? Cup me, bleed me, bring in the leeches. I can rid myself of my own blood, thank you and him. I go home tomorrow, I will say nothing of it."

"You go home to winter weather. It will be a stormy cold voyage."

"I go home to Christmas, sir. To the bosom of my family and the house decked with ivy and holly. Perhaps my—"

"No snivelling, damn you." He saw with disgust and a kind of relief to be anatomised later the sickly vignettes: his last Christmas, the cosseting of wet-eyed brave parents, death at the time of the daffodils, daffodils in the sick room, the military funeral, weeping Augusta at the grave with her fox-nose red, red-yarded Major Whoeveritwas saluting. Here lies Isaac Marmaduke.

IV

JOHN AWOKE TO THE BRIGHT DECEMBER MORNING COLD-
nosed and well, and he knew why. He had strapped on to a
soldierly back the burden of dying for love. This was not war,
this was not epidemic. Death did not like to be laughed at.
Its multiplication was not funny, but its duplication was side-
splitting. For himself and Elton to be spitting arterial blood
together would be the most comical thing in the world. One
deals a red ace, the other trumps it. Elton could attend to his
own death first; his, John Keats's, could follow at an uncomic
interval. Death would endeavour, in its glum way, to keep
things serious. He went into Severn's room. Severn was working on sketches for a painting to be called The Death of
Alcibiades. John said:

"You know what I said I would write?"

"A poem on the river Severn you said." Severn smiled up
with shy pleasure.

"Yes, full of sweet Severn and gently flowing Severn and
mighty Severn and Severn well-loved. Your name eternised in
verse and you to glory in adventitious fluminous attributes."

"I did not say that. I did not think that. I am pleased that
you think of working again. I should, of course, be pleased
also with a dedication."

"To Severn this poem on the Severn. That would never do.
I could of course write instead on the Tiber. The syllables are
the same, both names trochaic. The fluminous properties differ
little, though the history of what each river has borne upon its

back—well, no: men are men, battles battles, bridges bridges. I see little difference. *Tiber* has rhymes, at least I can think of one rhyme—fibre. A useful rhyme?"

"You must decide what is useful. You must decide whether to rhyme or no."

"Is that Alcibiades? He looks a little like Wordsworth."

"You mock, John."

"Seriously, I am here in Rome and I dream of English themes. Is that right?"

"You must decide."

"Let us imagine that William Shakespeare is brought here by his patron and friend the Earl of Southampton. It's possible, of course, that he was, and to Venice and Verona and Padua besides. What would he write?"

"The Rape of Lucrece?"

There was a knock at the apartment door, and John went to answer it. A sturdy young curled Roman, very ragged, his feet bare, smiled, pulled at a curl in humble greeting, held out a parcel roughly wrapped in newspaper, French for some reason, an old copy of the *Gazette de Francfort*. The lad said: "Misiter Kettis?"

"Approssimamente."

"Is lettera, misiter."

There was indeed. A note from Elton. With a book, a very big one. *Queen Anna's New World of Words*. The author John Florio. John's heart prepared to leap. He smiled at the boy and said: "So you speak some English?"

"Misiter Eliton a little a teach."

"And your name? *Come ti chiami?*"

"Mario." One of the surname-lacking poor. John felt in his pocket for a small coin. Mario thrust out his palms against the gift in horror, as again proffered violence. "Misiter Eliton he say a no. He say a Misiter Kettis *molto povero*."

"So it shows." John sighed. "Very poor, yes. Take this just the same." And then he had a remarkable vision. He saw this Mario as Marius, living by the Tiber while Rome was building, living through the growth and fall of the empire, always the same with his wine and bread and garlic, through two thousand years of the city's life. He gaped at the boy in awe. The boy said *grazie*, pulled a curl, ran. John leaned against the doorpost, trying to get breath back. The huge old book in his hands nearly slipped from them. Severn came out.

"Who was it? What is that? Are you well? You're pale. Is it bad news?"

"Not bad news, Severn. A present from Elton, that's all. Two presents from Elton, I think. I will lie down."

"Have you drunk your milk?"

"Some of it. I will drink the rest now. Lying down."

"But you're so pale."

"Not from weariness, Severn. Not that." And he went to lie down.

One thing at a time. He pushed from his head the vision of eternal Marius-Mario. He read Elton's note. "I take coach today. I woke well enough, though tired. No further you know what. I have taken much pleasure in our walks and talks together. Here is a farewell gift, a dictionary which I will no longer need since I am leaving Italy and am unlikely to return. It is very old, my great-grandfather had it. It is perhaps too old to be of use, but have it just the same. I will long remember the foul fustilugs and the business of the nose blowing, they will aid me when I am sad. A foul libel on the sex, sir, and the sex deserves it. Sincere good wishes from I. M. Elton, Lieut RE."

The book was intolerably heavy in his hands. He brought up his knees and made a lectern of them. LONDON, Printed by *Melch. Bradwood,* for *Edw. Blount* and *William Barret.* ANNO 1611. Year of the King James Bible. Shakespeare was how old? Forty-seven. With five years of life yet to run, he might have held this book, this very copy, in his hands, also finding it heavy. John's lectern-knees became Shakespeare's. John Florio had been Shakespeare's friend. At least he had been secretary to Shakespeare's noble dearmylove and patron.

Cazzo, *a man's priuie member. Also as* Cazzica.
Cazzolata, *a ladle-full. Also a musical instrument without*
strings.
Cazzo marino, *a Pintle-fish.*
Cazzo ritto, *a stiffe standing pricke.*
Cazzuto, *a man that hath a pricke.*

And a man that hath not? *Incazzuto,* perhaps. This is my dear friend, Signor Incazzuto. Apt for some play of Ben Jonson's, English humours in an Italian setting. Those worlds had been very close: the Italian realms and Elizabeth's own, or James's. No, with James they had begun to drift apart. Elizabeth or Elisabetta. She speaketh the Tuscan to perfection, my lord. Rightly is she named La Fiorentina.

He could not now, a minute after opening the book, recall whether he had opened at random or not. Cazzica, *an Interjection of admiration, what! gods me! god forbid, tush.* Tush, not to be superstitious, it was as though there might have been a sly Elizabethan guiding of his finger to *cazzo* and the rest that approval might in a manner thus be expressed from the shades of his translating that prick-naming sonnet. An interjection of admiration. He turned now to the back of the book, where Florio gave instructions as to the pronunciation of Italian:

> For so much as the Italians have two very different sounds for the two vowels E and O which for distinctions sake, they name the one close and the other open . . . The close E . . . is pronounced as the English E or Ea, as in these words, Bell, Beane, Den, Deane, Fell, Flea, Meade, Quell, Sell, Tell &c and the open E . . . is ever pronounced as Ai in English, as in these words Baile, Baine, Daine, Faile, Flaile, Maide, Quaile, Saile, Taile, &c . . .

It began to sunrise upon him slowly what this meant. It meant that he was being granted a vision (not the just word. Audition?) of how Shakespeare spoke. He spoke like an Irishman, *cazzica*. He said not *flea* but *flay*. He pronounced *reason* as *raisin*. And now it flashed in where the joke was in Falstaff's words: "reasons are as plentiful as blackberries." Of course, *raisins*. With awe and something of fear, John felt as if he were being instructed by the dead in person, souls of poets dead and gone. Doors were being opened. Welcome to long life and further revelations. The gods were accepting the blood sacrifice of Lieutenant Elton. He, John Keats, was being reserved for, preserved for—

He was on his feet, hands behind him, pacing from wall to wall when Dr Clark came in. Clark said: "Good morning," tossed a coin in his head it seemed and decided on Scotch. "Ye seem—restless, restive, unrested. Ye luik to me to hae a fever, mon."

"I am well, I never felt better. There are so many things I have to do. Let me tell you my—"

"Ye may tell Signor Gulielmi, wha's waiting for ye ootside. I hae nae time the noo for poetical blatherings. Weel, the starvation diet is haeing its effects. Ye are thinner though, aye."

"Being thin I conform the better to your view of how a consumptive should look. You never liked the appearance of unsick normality. I am hungry all the time, and I cannot think that to be good, I am damnably hungry."

"That's subjective, mon. But, to be objective, nae bleeding."

"No, no blood comes up. Or down."

"Weel then, that is because of the licht diet. Persevere, and ye may weel soon be like Lieutenant Elton, the blood-spitting gone and he on his way hame."

"I shall end up here, sick or well, dead or living. I think Rome and I have things to say to each ither, other."

Clark waved that away as of no moment. "Gulielmi has a mind to take ye to see Roman things, meet Roman folk forbye. We'll gang doon together." He suddenly grew weary of Scotch, it seemed, as of a language it required concentration to speak, a sort of Italian. "It is not all that warm outside. The sun is a deceiver. Take your topcoat." John listened with interest to the patrician accent. He caught a flash of Clark in high places, a physician to the nobility perhaps, saw him in a gilded bedroom with a scutcheon over the bed, but heard comforting Scotch treacling out like a placebo: *Aye, aye, ye rest yon heid the noo, yer grace.*

"Aye," John said.

Gulielmi, raw northern bones and droll Roman eyes, drably dressed for the bright day, smiled faintly at a mother seated on the Spanish Steps, giving her great breast to a boy who was surely more than ready for weaning. Both wore costumes of the Campagna, artist's models both. The Steps were a lolling minced rainbow of artist's models, and there were also the flowersellers. The church bell sang once, and in some strange way it embraced the scene. John saw why, and his heart jumped. The whirring fragments of sound that splintered off from the bell's main note were those colours, and the fundamental bongggg was white. Colours whirred or whirled into God's white and away and back again. What did God have to do with anything? No, here in Rome you could not say that. There was room for Apollo and Venus and still some for God. He tasted the faint aloes of resentment at the hunched coughing narrow-chested God of the English.

"Mr Keats," Gulielmi greeted, "I see the rose of health on thy cheek."

"Master Kates, Shakespeare would call me. I have had the revelation this morning of hearing Shakespeare's voice. Florio's Dictionary. I have learned that Shakespeare said *tête* for *tail* and *mêde* for *maid*. Their sounds were not ours, they were European sounds. I wonder if Shakespeare was ever in Rome."

"Well, he was closer to Rome, and to Veneto, and to the whole of Italy than any of your poets have been since, Mr Shelley and Lord Byron not excepted. England seems more and more to move away from Europe. Speaking of moving, do you feel yourself well enough to move by ferry and carrozza to the Cappella Sistina?"

"Not too much excitement," Dr Clark answered for John. "Let us no undo the salvatory work of the light diet. Fish. If there is to be dinner, let it be fish."

"Fish, yes. But Michelangelo before the fish," Gulielmi said.

"Michelangelo is unco' exciting." And Dr Clark fussed off to see other patients. Gulielmi hailed a carrozza on the Corso, telling the rogue of a driver to drive to the Porto de Ripetta ferry. John's supply of breath was not enough to sustain the skyboat of his enthusiasms. He tried to tell Gulielmi about the idea within himself that was trying to attain the first crude crudely workable shape, the—"Blobs of mercury—being brought together—by some helpful fingertip—to form the one—quicksilver disc—"

"Calm. You must be calm. It is good for you to be calm."

So John saved his breath and took in the Romans—workmen, carriers, barefoot child beggars skilled in adult obscenity: *cazzo . . . coglioni . . . puttana . . . vafnculo.* He would have to start reading hard. He would have to think of a stanza form. Blank verse, rhymed couplets, no. *Terza rima?* But that would seem like a mockery of Dante. The sonnet used as a stanza? That meant each phase of the story would thud or sweep or sidle in like a wave, then recoil. And why not? The octave for the public event, the sestet for the unchanging Marius or Mario. Unchanging, there was the rub. Could you really compose a lengthy poem about what never changed? His heart began to sink, and he recognised that, in a manner, his survival depended on the right burgeoning of this poetic idea. But to what category did the idea, would the poem, belong? Tragedy? Hardly, great men dying but a small man eternally remaining. Was he capable of it? It was some new thing, some category to be freshly invented. It was not the comic of *Don Juan,* not squibbish and irreverent. It was mightily reverent to this persistent Roman. Yet (heart dropping further, awareness of light flooding his eyes as his eyes further widened) what does Marius-Mario do but persist in living, begetting, working, owing rent, borrowing, drinking? He does not move, he does not generate a narrative.

They had been set down in the piazza of St Peter. "You look pale," Gulielmi said. "You need some grape spirit." And he led him, hand gently on his arm, to a wineshop off the square, cave-like, dusty, not warm.

"It tastes," John said, when he had sipped a little, "not unlike the way an old dog smells."

"It will do you no harm."

"I'm trying to bring to birth a long poem which shall some-how celebrate Rome. I'm disturbed by certain difficulties, and I cannot afford to be so disturbed, not now, not not now."

"Tell me the subject." Gulielmi looked grave as he listened.

"You see, for the first time in the history of poetry we have a common man, an ordinary soul—with Wordsworth you have peasants and shepherds but the poet imposes on them his own metaphysic. He pretends to present the speech of ordi-nary men, but does not. Here, through a common Roman—"

He stopped, in evident distress. Gulielmi waited. Then he said: "Go on."

"How could an Englishman do it? The ordinary speech of Romans is to be set down by Romans, not by Englishmen." The sudden distress seemed to make him thinner and smaller. He hunched over his little glass of grappa as to draw warmth from it. Gulielmi wished to say, but dared not: *It is not for you, this thing is reserved for another. The muse presiding over this notion has hit the wrong season and the wrong poet.* Aware of the depth the despondency could reach and of its danger, he said instead:

"Most fine notions begin in despair. This you must know. There is a whole wing of your mind's mansion unknown to you, where, as it were, work is already proceeding on your notion. A thousand clerks are scratching away. Or shall we imagine that it is the headquarters of a Grand Army of the poetic imagination, with some inner Napoleon plotting with his staff, maps spread, dividers calculating the day's march, while a whole corps awaits its orders. You must not think of this again, not with your brain of the daylight. Let us go and see Michelangelo."

John's face seemed to fill out again and the rose returned. He smiled, though ruefully, and let the last drop of dog-smelling grappa fall on to his tongue. He said:

"How old was Michelangelo when he died?"

"Ridiculously old. In his nineties and working till the end. But he felt he had learned nothing of his art. If he had lived to one hundred and ninety he would perhaps have felt the same."

"The life so short, the art so long to learn. I have done nothing."

"His very words. Come."

They entered the chapel by way of the Stradone dei Giardini. A guard responded to Gulielmi's triple knock and they were almost at once set upon by Michelangelo. It tired John to throw back his head, like a hen drinking, to be drowned by the muscular ceiling. He concentrated on the Last Judgment. "It is very fine," he said politely. "But not very Christian."

"It is a statement of Christian doctrine. Christ shall say to the wicked: *Depart from me ye cursed into everlasting fire—*"

"Yes, I know of that, Godless one as I am. But he also welcomes the blessed into everlasting bliss. Where are the blessed?"

"There you see them. There, you see, is the flayed Saint Bartholomew, and the skin he is holding is the skin of Michelangelo himself. You see the ghost of his face in the skin. That is very much a self-portrait."

"There are no signs of blessedness. It is all horror. All hell. Nor is that the Christ they teach of in the churches. Look at his great muscles. Look at his bearded ferocity. He is more Prometheus than Christ, except that he has no love of mankind. He does not bring us fire, he throws us into it. Where did he get those huge shoulder muscles? Not from a year or so of work in a carpenter's shop."

"*San Bartolomeo,*" a voice said behind them. "*Lui stesso.*" They turned. John saw a neat young swarthy man with one bigger and tougher, great-eyed, ebon-locked, mustachioed. This latter was carrying a sevenbranched candlestick, the seven flames dancing in unison to a breeze that wafted through the chapel. Gulielmi said:

"Belli. Giuseppe Gioacchino Belli, *poeta.* John Keats, *poeta.*" The two poets piacered each other warily. Belli was gorgeously decked in the flames of his candles, all gold and shadow and face-caves. Belli said:

"Don Valentino Llanos." A Spaniard, then. The Spaniard bowed. He said in very fair English:

"A poet from England? I am most happy." His aspirate had the swift throatiness of a jota. "Your name again, sir?"

"Keats."

"But I know your work," Llanos said in delight. "'Much have I travelled in the realms of gold.'" A Spanish roundness in that *gold,* the *jav* and the *trav* true rhymes, a slack *b* quality in the *v.* And the *much* a truncated *mucho.* He, John Keats, had travelled to the realms of gold. "I study the poets of England. I am happier to meet a poet alive than a painter dead. I shall ever remember meeting Mr Keats under the Day of Judgment."

"Better under than on." He despised himself for the joke in the act of making it. "All Don Juans go the same way."

"But this is no true hell. It is as it were all pure energy with nothing of sin or judgment about it."

"I first saw it as terrifying, now as absurd. The painter has filled it with his own guilt. I can guess at the nature of the guilt, I think. He was too fond of broadshouldered boys."

Meanwhile Gulielmi spoke to Belli.

"You were where?"

"In the Marche."

"You saw young Leopardi?"

"Leopardi, no. Not Leopardi."

"So. I ask no more questions. Is your Laura turning you into a Petrarch?"

"Do not joke, friend. I will show you what she has inspired. You will not grin then."

"Sonnets?"

"And more than sonnets."

John said to Llanos: "My last unfinished poem was, I suppose, about Michelangelo giants. Ponderous. It will not now be finished and I have few regrets. Michelangelo cures through his pretensions pretensions of our own. I am sick of big men. I would write of little ones if I could."

"Why are you here in Rome? You join the exiles like myself?"

"A matter of my health, señor. I have offended no tyrant, I think."

Belli was saying to Gulielmi: "What is his name again? Kettis? Kattis? These English names are impossible." John heard that and said:

"Keats, signore, Keats. You have the combination of sounds already in your language. As in *cazzo,* as in *cazzica.*"

Belli emitted a long mouthful at that, which John understood to convey the shock Belli felt at the impropriety of the employment of such language in a holy place before and under holy pictures.

"*Mi dispiace, mi dispiace, molto.* I am a horrible obscene irreligious Englishman and *mi dispiace moltissimo.*" That mollified Belli somewhat but reproof, dramatised by his flapping candle flames, rested in the fine eyes.

"Signor Belli," Gulielmi explained to John, "is, shall we say, professionally prone to sensitivity about these matters. He is a papal officer, you see, and is sometimes assigned to the duty of showing distinguished visitors the holy art of our city. However, what you would wish to do now, I think, is to rest. We shall go to my apartment in Trastevere. I will go out and send some urchin for a carrozza."

"Michelangelo," John said, "does seem somewhat to breathe all the available air. But I am, believe me, grateful for this opportunity to see his masterpieces. They are a terrible warning."

"*Un ammonimento spaventoso,*" Gulielmi tranlated. Belli nodded, his great eyes full of candles, and beat his breast thrice to the loud bassoon of the Judgment.

V

BELLI HAD SPOKEN FRENCH BUT NOW, FOR SOME REASON,
clung to Italian, Tuscan mostly but sometimes Roman. He spoke
the Roman in a strange mixed tone of shame and defiance. He
said something about Dante and Gulielmi translated.

"Michelangelo knew Dante by heart. Any good Italian
poet knows Dante by heart. Any good poet anywhere knows
some Dante by heart. Do *you* know any of Dante by heart?"

"The opening lines of the *Inferno.*"

"Let us, he says, hear them from your English mouth."

John recited, with near-Elizabethan vowels:

> "*Nel mezzo del cammin di nostra vita*
> *Mi ritrovai per una selva oscura*
> *Che la diritta via era smarrita.*"

Llanos, who was at supper with them, gave John a *bravo;*
Belli merely grunted. Then he recited, roughly and defiantly:

> "*A mitaa strada de quell gran viacc*
> *Che femm a vun la voeulta al mondo da la*
> *Me sont trovata in d'on bosch scur scur affacc,*
> *Senza on sentee da pode seguita.*"

"What language is that?" John asked.

"Italian. Another kind of Italian. The dialect of Milan. And
that is Carlo Porta's translation of those lines of Dante into the

tongue of the common people of Milan." Belli added a sort of growl of challenge.

John did not truly know what response was expected of him. He cut his tough veal and chewed. They were in a tavern in a low street off the Corso. A meat meal and to the temporary devil with Dr Clark's bloodless diet. And the wine they had now was red and ferrous as ink, all the way from Piedmont. John had eaten an obedient small portion of fish that afternoon in Gulielmi's house and spent two hours trying to explain certain passages in his Odes, which Gulielmi wished to translate into Italian, meaning Tuscan. Then he had rested and tried not to think of the agonies already springing like warts from the long poem he had to write. Yet he knew that something must go down on paper soon. It was a matter of choosing between two thick fluids.

Belli said something and Gulielmi translated.

"You would call yourselves in England a unified people with a unified people's unified language?"

"A matter of being a kingdom and what is known as the King's English, though our kings are German. All printed books are in that English. Save for the few poets who write in Scotch."

"Your king is the head of your church?"

"He is the head of the Church of England, yes."

"If you have a Church of England then you have a God of England. Your so-called Reformation cut you off from the family of Europe. Like the other snorting and hawking peoples of the North." Gulielmi said: "The words are stronger in Roman. Snorting and hawking will do, though. I apologise," he added.

"You mean the God of Italy?" John said. "Cut us off from

that, him? You say the North, but till Bonaparte brought God back to France France lived for some few happy years with a naked Goddess of Reason." John felt uncomfortable talking of God, more uncomfortable hearing his words about God put into Italian while Belli listened with gravity. Was it true gravity or an enacted one? Was Belli drunk? The thin sharp Roman wine had micturated round freely before his Piedmontese ink had begun its slower inscriptions. Who or what was this Belli, besides some vague official of the papacy? If a poet, what kind of poet? A writer of hymns?

"*Inni?*" Belli had a harsh laugh at that. And then he grew too swiftly grave again. "In a sense perhaps. Hymns to beauty, to love, to the Platonic essences. Little holy hymns we leave to Fra Sperandio."

"Who?"

"Fra Sperandio," Llanos said. "Brother Trustgod, Godtrust."

"God trussed up in glib poetaster pieties. I see. I know nothing of God or faith or churches," John said. "I believe in the holiness of the human imagination, the brotherhood of all elements of the cosmos, the creation of the human soul through suffering and love, the divine revelations of poetry."

That sounded imposing in Tuscan. Belli spat something small on to the floor. "The goodness of man? Man's innate goodness?"

"If man is not good, it is because he has not yet learned to be good. He can learn, however. Perhaps he is learning already."

"So man is born good?"

"He is born neither good nor bad." And then: "I am not even sure what the words mean. So many of our troubles spring from Nature, not from the actions of men. Or women." He almost put an urgent hand on Gulielmi's arm, to stem his translating. This translating of everything made everything seem like something sworn on oath, or printed, given to the *Edinburgh Review,* to sneer at. Llanos, bored rightly, was telling the host of the tavern how veal was cooked in Madrid and district, Gulielmi had turned into a mere translation engine, Belli was John's only audience; still, commit words even to the empty air and you were committing your soul to some ultimate judgment, Apollonian perhaps, nothing to do with the Michelangelesque nightmare. Poetry was different; poetry was not judged in terms of sense and nonsense, except by the *Edinburgh Review.* Belli seemed to carry with him the disturbing listening emptiness of a hypothetical futurity. John began to sweat. He sweated more when he saw something in the undoored kitchen at the room's end: a slattern, wiping her red hands after washing trenchers, seized eagerly by the waiting-lout and fumbled: a bare bosom flashed, strawberry-nippled, and was pawed. She ran, giggling, he ran after. John sweated.

The host, fat, though with a greyish face scored by deep and dusty runnels, kept saying "*Sí, sí, sí*" to indulge Llanos, unconvincible as to the virtue of the Madrid way. But then he said something rapid and coarse, full of Roman noises. Llanos laughed. "What was that?" John asked. "What makes you laugh so?"

Belli was saying in a sort of horrified fascinated trance: "*. . . Cuesti cqui sso rreliquioni—ma ar mi' paese . . .*"

"Why, yes," Llanos said, surprised. "Those very words. It must be some old Roman saying about Spaniards. 'Here in Rome we have Adam's balls.'—'Ah, but we in Spain have Adam's—' "

"*Cazzo,*" John said, too loudly. Eaters turned unamused, to hear a foreigner use a dirty word, a Roman's privilege.

Belli had heard John on Nature, through Gulielmi, as well as the coarse host. He was a listening man, so much was evident: he made use of his two ears. He spoke long and bitterly. Gulielmi said: "He says that you free-thinking Protestant English poets have forgotten how to think, freely or otherwise. Excuse me—this is his view, not, as you know, necessarily mine. Free thinking, he says, is anyway no thinking. You have substituted something called Nature for God, and with Nature there is nothing but Truth and Beauty and Goodness till you fall sick, and then Nature becomes lying and ugly and malevolent. You make Nature both God and devil, but it is the one or the other only according to your moods."

"I did not say that," John said lamely. "I do not think that. As for falling sick, what does he know about my falling sick?"

"He says you are evidently and very clearly sick. I think, as you know, you are better today, but he will have it that you are sick."

Belli looked at John grimly during this, great dark eyes trained on a sick English poet who did not know how to think.

"He also says that man is born evil."

"Why?" John asked, sweating worse than ever.

Belli knew the word. *"Perché, perché, perché?"* he said in crescendo, and then much of which John could understand little.

"*Why* won't unwrite the book, he says. He says those of you who reject the traditional view of man, which is not only Christian but also Jewish and Musulman, those, he says, must write their own book. You will find plenty of material he says, forgive me, up the arsehole of Pasquino's statue."

"Pasquino?"

"A bust, not a statue," Llanos said. "On the Via di Pasquino near the Piazza Navona. It is where anonymous lampoons are placed. Satirical verses. You will have seen it."

"I've seen nothing," John said. "I know nothing." He felt sick and weary and began to taste, with a disquiet that made the sweat gush, a rusty gob that was sliding up to his mouth. Covertly he spat it into his handkerchief, covertly looked. Thank God or Nature, there was no red. The taste of rust was the taste of the wine from Piedmont. His relief was immense. Stowing the handkerchief in his breast, he found there the coda'd sonnet about the dumpendebat. "This," he said to Gulielmi, smiling, "is for you."

Gulielmi took it, saw what it was, hastily handed it back. "Not now. Perhaps tomorrow."

"No, no. Take it home, read at leisure."

Belli was quick to see it was a poem neatly engrossed in green ink. *"Un altro sonetto,"* he said, his nostrils widening. *"Su un altro gatto?"*

John understood that. "Not cats," he said. *"Cazzi."*

Belli jerked it out of Gulielmi's hand rudely, then scanned it. He would know no more than that it was a sonnet with a coda. About *cazzi*. He peered closely at it however and hit a word thrice with his index finger. *"Dumpendebat,"* he said bitterly to Gulielmi. Then he raged at Gulielmi very finely, so that the room stopped eating to listen, using most expressive gestures of his fine ringed hands, and Gulielmi was apologetic and humble, flashing odd brief looks of hurt at John. Belli got up, tore the poem in two, four, eight, snowing the fragments over the dirty dishes. He swished up his grey cloak from the back of his chair, nearly sending flying a full wine jug on the neighbour table. The neighbour

eater saved his jug with both hands, barking Romanly, eyes
abulge, while the wine danced to its resettling. Belli grabbed his
hat from the chairpost and slammed it on his black locks.

"That," John said, "is mine. That is discourteous." Belli,
bowing only to Llanos, strode out in what seemed to be a rage-
engendered gale that bore his cloak-folds aloft. "Well," John
said. "He wrings at some distress."

"It was he," Gulielmi said, "who wrote the original. You
translated what he wrote."

"I did not know. How could I know?"

"I told you the author had destroyed it in anger and shame.
He did not know that I had a copy."

"Anger and shame—why? It is a mere bawdy joke. It is the
sort of thing any poet will do in fun. It is somewhat childish to
be angry and ashamed."

"You will never understand Belli," Gulielmi sighed. "Nor,
I think, will I. He is like two men always fighting each other.
Most men learn to come to terms with their higher and lower
selves. After all, we are all equipped with an apparatus of gen-
eration, and we all have aspirations to the pure life of the soul.
But Belli is not satisfied with how God made him, which seems
to mean that he is not satisfied with God, and this feeds an
evergrowing guilt."

"He is married?" Llanos asked.

"He married a widow of some wealth, and he is both joyful
and guilty about that. His childhood was poor and unhappy,
and the poverty and unhappiness should, so his strange scheme
of justice would have it, both continue and not continue. He
is unfaithful, I think, but not physically. He has a Beatrice or
Laura somewhere in the Marche, and he writes her the most
spiritual poems."

"I am sorry to say," Llanos said, "that he does not write well. Not that I have seen much of what he has written."

"I think he does write well," Gulielmi said, "though not supremely well. But as he is torn between his soul and his lower instincts, so is he also torn between the language of Petrarch or Dante and the rough speech he hears all about him in Rome. He has seen what Carlo Porta can do with the language of the Milan streets. He feels, I think, that he may have a duty to the low and dirty language of his native city. But that language, as you are perhaps a little learning, Mr Keats, is not the language of the soul."

"His," Llanos said, "was one of the names I was given. The name of an opener of doors, very friendly with cardinals." It was as though he thought it was time to be apologising for knowing Belli.

"Well," John said, "I cannot expect him to listen to me now, but I could have counselled him to a way out of his guilt and unhappiness. The way out is the way out of the conception of ourselves as unified beings. We are, in fact, unities in name and appearance and voice and a set of habits only. We are nothing more, and to flesh ourselves with character we must identify ourselves, swiftly, temporarily, with one or other of our brothers and sisters of the universe. We have to dress up in the borrowed raiment of a comet, the moon, a pecking sparrow, a snowflake, boiling water, a billiard ball rolling towards a pocket. The dumpendebat self of our friend and the stabat mater self are but two among the many selves available. I see, though, that this atomising of the self would never appeal. It is not very Christian. But then I do not believe in the existence of art that is Christian. Art is not anything but art."

"You have Michelangelo in your mind, I think," Llanos faintly smiled. "And the thought also that it is not Signor Belli's soul that must be saved but his art."

"How else can a man save his soul save through art of some kind or other? A saint's life, I suppose, is a kind of art, in which the material is not stone or words or paint but conduct. And it is in the saint's art like the poet's that we that we—" The slattern and the serving-lout had returned to the kitchen from somewhere dark at the back, no longer fumbling and fumbled, sleek, rather, if sleekness was at all possible to two such, sleek as street cats could sometimes be—

"The saint's art?" said Gulielmi.

"Forgive me, I was distracted. I was thinking of the putting off of self and the striving to live inside other beings. St Francis of Assisi perhaps was such a saint-artist. And Signor Belli perhaps," he smiled now, "has the makings possibly of a kind of saint. He worries enough to be a saint. I must go home," he coda'd. "You will forgive my unseasonable tiredness. It has been a long day. But a pleasant one, an instructive one," he quickly added.

"Perhaps you walked too much. If so it is my fault." Gulielmi was, it seemed, in a mood to be guilty about everything. "Tomorrow I go north," he said gloomily. "A matter of some small property near Pisa." He seemed prepared to dredge guilt out of owning a small property, out of the prospect of travel on its behoof. "I may see your friend Mr Shelley there. We have had some correspondence about his play *The Cenci*. It may or may not be translatable. It is about incest." He reached the bottom of gloom and began to rise. "We shall meet again," he said. "In the new year. And crack something together."

"Crack?" Llanos said.

"A bottle. You too, Don Valentino. If you are still to be here."

"Oh yes, I shall be here. The times are not yet auspicious for my return to Spain. There is a certain— It is repressive in Spain just now. It is not very liberal. I will come to see you," he said to John, "on, ha, appropriate, the Spanish Steps, if I may. There is much interest in Spain," he added, "in the poets of England."

"In England we all love Don Quixote."

So, very amicable together, separating, they separated. John walked home, thinking. Tomorrow he must make a start, must. Heroic couplets perhaps, after all. And personal, a personal beginning. Here I am in Rome and a boy called Mario came, and I thought, the eternal Roman. And my mind went back to, and I do in my own way what Shakespeare did, the murder of Julius Caesar, and Marius saw it and ran home, afraid. And. It was not really what he had in mind, though. Something carved, not flowing. He would write anyway, he would make a beginning.

Beneath an ilex on a hill of Rome
At sunset I gazed down upon the dome
Of Buonarroti crowning Peter's fane—

This will never do, back to your gallipots. Thinking, frowning, arms behind him, hands tight clasped, hat pushed back from brow, he came to with a great start crossing the Corso. His heart leaped, fell, thudded. Eight hooves stumbled and clattered recovering, two bay horses' heads were reined back, there was a double whinneying, the horses' bull-eyes looked down in horror surely exaggerated. The Roman coachman was very loud with dirty words, his whip raised as if to lash John. The flames in the coachlamps danced, the coach rocked, the liveried tiger at the rear booed and made tearing gestures. *"Mi dispiace,"* John said. A lady put her head out.

"Che succede?"

John realised that he was, thank Bacchus, not untipsy. He swept off his hat and bowed courtlily low, saying:

"Alma Venus."

Pauline Bonaparte, the Princess Borghese, pallidly beautiful under the faint moon that Horace and Vergil had known, only a little engulesed by the capering lampflame, rested one delicate hand on the crest of the coat of arms that was gilded on the coach door. She was in a ballgown of turquoise, her hair flashed with gems, her kashmir wrap had fallen some way back off her glowing shoulders. Her perfume was heavy and somewhat spicy, as if she were to be eaten. She recognised John. She said something in rapid Corsican Italian which, for all John knew, could be about his being a wretched wight alone and palely loitering. But she smiled, her eyes smiled. *"Votre ami,"* she said more slowly. *"Votre bel ami."*

"Parti, madame. Je le regrette. Hélas, hélas, parti."

"Qui êtes-vous, monsieur?"

"Un poète anglais, madame. Le nom n'importe rien. Le nom ne vivra guère. Scritto," he added, *"in acqua."*

"Voulez-vous profiter de mon carrosse, monsieur?"

What was that word? Did it mean caress? Did he wish to profit from her caress? What was she saying?

"Merci bien, madame, vous êtes gentille. Mais—" And, for lack of the right words, he gestured that he lived near and was well able to walk thither. He bowed, she inclined her beautiful

smiling gemmed head, she nodded to the coachman to proceed. John stood, watching. *Carrosse* meant coach. The coach
proceeded.

He awoke that night much disturbed. Healthy, even strong,
the strength of grilled veal in his arteries. He awoke to physical desire from a dream in which he was on the point of
fulfilling it. His dear girl, F.B., leered at him naked in some
tent of blue satin reeking of hyacinths, her breasts bigger
naked than he had known them clothed, her rounded arms
seeking him as though blindly, though her eyes were open,
dilated, full of lust. His main aim in the dream, it appeared,
was to shut those eyes, which he did, with kiss after kiss,
so that his head went into the clickclock of the Haydn
slow movement Severn had once played. The eyelids accepted
the kisses but were quick to open again after each, and
his kisses engaged fluttering lashes before lids. He closed his
own eyes then and put his lips to hers and seemed to start to
tumble towards a dark hyacinth-reeking membranous pit.
John Florio read aloud from his *World of Words* as from a
bible. He cackled *"Fica"* in the imagined voice of Robert
Burton. "A figge. Also used for a woman's quaint." So that
explained the Marvell line about her quaint honour turning
to dust. Shakespeare was there, picking it seemed fig-seeds
from bad teeth with a new-cut swan-quill. He nodded. It was
a signal to spend seed, and John cried *no no*, hurtling himself
back to waking. The church clock chimed a quarter.

He lay nursing a rod gone flaccid, listening to the song
of the fountain in the piazza. He thought he knew now why
Belli was angry and ashamed to have written that sonnet. The
danger of play. One offended the gods at one's peril. The caress
was a carrosse to the dark world.

Stabat mater dolorosa
Apud lignum lachrymosa
Dum pendebat filius.

He had touched nothing of poetry, nothing, save in odd single lines he did not well understand. Pretty tales, gods and nymphs stolen from the marbles Elgin stole. Meanwhile a body hung on a cross and a mother wept. Play. Sonnet competitions over the teacups in Leigh Hunt's untidy house. Crowning each other with laurels: play. Apollo was not amused, was not mocked. John sweated in fear and prayed: "Whoever presides over poetry, spare me to dare the darkness. Everything is an allegory of the unknown. Teach me the way of the reading of the signs. Give me time to grow. I promise faithful service. No more play." Then he fell into heavy sleep.

VI

⌒

SEVERN CAME EARLY THE NEXT MORNING TO JOHN'S ROOM.
He had been out in the cool sunlight to post a letter to Will
Haslam. It had been on Haslam's recommendation that John
had come here, Haslam was a true friend who would be happy
to learn that the advice had proved sound, that John was
stronger in body and as active as ever in mind. A hopeful letter, then, and hope was confirmed in Severn as he found John
awake, sitting up in bed and scribbling. He had made a knee
desk of a big old book whose faded title Severn could roughly
make out—*A Word of Worlds* or something. John had paper
and a newly cut quill. On the chair beside his bed were the
penknife, the inkwell, the drained milk cup of the previous
day. John's eyes were bright, his cheeks healthily, so it seemed,
flushed. His redgold hair was uncombed.

"Sabrina fair, how is the Roman morning?"

"I saw a very pretty little crib outside a church whose
name I forget, with a little chubby Jesus child choked in tinsel.
The Romans are already thinking of Christmas. It is but two
weeks to go now. You stayed out yesterday. You should have
said you would not be home for dinner. As we have to pay for
two I ate two. I was dyspeptic. Signora Angeletti gave me some
bubbling fountain water. It helped."

"Bubbling Severn. I am bubbling too, words are bubbling.
I had this mad notion yesterday of a long poem on Rome, the
history of Rome and the unchangingness of the Roman. Then

I woke in the night and it was, lo, revealed unto me that such a tale must be in prose. It is not for me, then."

"So what are you writing?"

"For the moment I am succumbing to madness and revelling in it. I am back to the notion of a river, though it is not necessarily the Severn. It might well be the Jordan. I am letting the river carry everything on his back, or hers. I see the river, though, as very male. See what I have done, and if you laugh I shall be pleased."

Severn took the sheet and read:

A bearded corpse, a corpse with lesser beard,
Father and son, hands death-clasped, as they feared
The river's disuniting, and, above,
Swooping through clouds, the ghost of a black dove,
And cleft by rocks a melon with black teeth,
While an old signpost rose from underneath
The joyous waters, with outlandish script
I could not read. Then, with their grey hides stripped
As from an ancient beating, bloated dogs
Sailed on their backs . . .

"I cannot very well laugh at something I fail altogether to understand."

"I do not understand it either," John said cheerfully. "But it is not the poet's task to be clear, even to the poet. Hens lay eggs but can say nothing of the richness of yolk and airy blandness of albumen. Talking of eggs, I think I could—" Then he started to cough. He shrugged at it, coughing, as at a transient nuisance. Then the coughing increased and became paroxysmal.

John's eyes showed fear, his nails grappled *A World of Words* in panic. Severn breathed fast and shallow. Scarlet gushed out and John moaned, choking. He tried madly to use his manuscript as a cup. The inky quill fell from the knee desk and wrote briefly on the coverlet. Severn was quick with the cup that had held milk. John filled it and groaned "Oh God God." There was a thick bubbling in his chest, then throat. Severn opened the casement and threw the rich red out like slops. He shut it again against the mild chill and was in time to offer the vessel for another filling of crimson. Severn looked at it fascinated and said calmly:

"I must get Clark." There was no more gushing, merely a few blobs and strings of phlegmy red to lace the brimming cup. John lay back, wretched, ashamed, fearful, disappointed. "I will go find him now. Or I will ask Signora Angeletti." There was no blood, though the breathing rattled, now, two cups enough, more than. John lay back very pale.

"You fetch him. We do not want. This is our little. Play."

"I'll wait. I'll wait five minutes."

"There'll be no more. Not yet. Get him. Though what he can do I. Know not. We must fulfill. The prop prop." *A World of Words* fell ponderously to the floor. "I'm cold. I must have blankets. Or a."

"I'll light a fire when I get back. Huddle under the clothes. Our two greatcoats will help. I shall be back in no time."

Clark, when he came, said nothing. He shook his head sadly at John and then nodded encouragingly. Meanwhile Severn, with old newspapers, candle ends, twigs, branchlets, tried to make a fire in the small grate. "Relieve inflammation," Clark said three or four times like a cantrip. Meanwhile he got some spirit alight with a spill from Severn's fire. He swirled the spirit about in a glass cup he had taken from his bag.

"Have I not already. Lost enough. Blood to relieve."

"Rest. Dinna, don't tire yoursel, self."

Clark clamped the heated cup with its roughened edges to the skin of John's left forearm. It adhered. It cooled. The air it held contracted. Surprised at the diminution of the surface pressure, deep-seated blood rose to the skin. Clark removed the cup, took his knife, incised. Blood came royally up, richly red.

"I have proof. It is not my. Stomach. The blood that came up had. Air bubbles. Air."

"It gathered that on its journey frae the stomach. Rest." He packed his bag, grinned at Severn's smoky troubles, then said seriously to John: "Excitement. Michelangelo and wine, I doot not. Blathering aboot poetry. There'll be no more of that for a wee while. I'll be back." Then he went clattering down the marble stairs. Severn, looking up from his little flames, was very surprised to see John out of the bed, tottering, scarlet and grey phlegm on his nightshirt like paint on a smock.

"No more, Severn. This is my. Last day."

Severn was up then and with him, fighting him with some difficulty, God knew where he got the strength from, bled out as he was. "What is it you're after, what are you seeking? Back to bed, John, you've lost enough—"

The great rabid eyes lighted on the penknife and flashed. "If you won't. Let me have my." Severn got the knife first. "Laudanum. Laudanum."

"Into that bed, into it. I have no laudanum. Clark has your laudanum." John fainted, falling on the bed, then almost at once recovered. He was persuaded to lie in it. Severn added blankets from his own bed. The fire crackled feebly. John lay awake with his eyes shut.

"John, listen to me, John, you are not to think of that wickedness. I know you've thought of it before, you thought of it even on the voyage. There will be no point in your looking for the means of self-destruction, do you hear me? There will be no knives or scissors or razors about, do you hear me? You are to lie still and get well."

"I'll not get well, Severn. This day shall be my last."

"A man does not take his own life. The law of Christ and the civil codes of the world alike forbid it. Be calm. I'll bring you milk. The room will be warm soon, you will see."

"Oh, damn and bugger your civil code and your cold Christ, Severn. I want no more of this. Dying in bloody cack and sweat and shivers. I think of you as well as of myself." The clarity and energy of his articulation were surprising. Severn looked at the clear open rolling eyes with awe, penknife in his fist. "Do you want that then, weeks maybe months, wiping up shit and blood and vomit? Let me be out of it like a." He grinned viciously. "I am more an antique Roman than a. It's easy enough, the quietus, Severn. The wrist-cutting is messy, throat-cutting too much Drury Lane. I ask only laudanum. A sufficient dose and tuck me in for the night. I will pass and you will scarce notice. I will void bladder and bowels like a good boy first. Give it to me, Severn."

"I told you, I no longer have it, Clark has it."

"Well, fuck, fuck, it is in shops, it is in druggists. God knows we have hardly enough money left for living but there must be enough for the other commodity. There is a druggist's shop on the Corso, very near to here. Get it for me, Severn."

"You know I cannot. It would be a kind of murder."

"This is the true murder, Severn. Must I abide this murder by the evil spirits in control? It is a human duty to cheat them."

"You're raving, John. It is the lack of blood. You must rest, you must, truly."

"I desire rest, can you not see that, damned fool? I am not permitted rest. The malignancies are on me."

"You must respect my faith, John. The Lord forbids suicide. He forbids the abetting of suicide. It is the final wickedness, to take one's own life."

"Your damnable Lord did it. He knew he was to die and he did not avoid it. He did not wish to escape. He let himself be crucified. I call that self-slaughter."

"He was killed by the Jews and the Romans. And he rose from the dead. We all rise, remember that. There is life after death for us all. But we forfeit that resurrection through grave sin. There is no sin graver than—"

"You believe this. I do not. My ghost be with the old philosophers." He was better. The blood loss had cleared his brain. He was ready, mad as it all was, for intellectual argument.

"Because you do not believe it does not mean it is not all true. If I do not believe that Florence or Naples exists it does not prevent their existing. Eternal life, eternal damnation— these are real, whether you believe or not." John listened to that. "Now rest," Severn said. John howled out:

"Brainless fool. There are men come back from Florence. We have smelt Naples, stinking hole of sea rats. There is no traveller back from your. After this there is nothing but a great blackness and I wish to engage it today, now. My body to the worms and what is human in me to what of humanity may take it. I am all disease, Severn, and disease is to be burnt out. I am a living tumour, a kind of devil. Fuck and shit to your lying gentle Jesus and your stupid false hopes. If you will not buy me laudanum I will buy it myself." And he got out of bed, despite Severn's pushing of him back into it. He fought hard with Severn, gasping raucously, and even got as far as his stockings, which lay on a chair with his shirt and breeches. Tottering and hopping to get one stocking on, he nearly fell into the fire which, feeble yet, could scarcely harm him. "I cannot," he panted. "I must wait till the blood is back in me. You will not?"

"Buy you laudanum, no. No and always no. Do not expect me to weaken on this. Back into bed with you."

John lay again, sweating coldly, cursing quietly in the monotone of liturgy. Severn tended his fire, which began to chew languidly at green pine. Then he sat on a plain green rickety chair by the fire, his hands loosely joined, praying, fearful eyes on John. John's eyes were on the pale flowers of the wallpaper. "They do not know," he said, "any of them, what mischief they do when they bring a child into the world. They allow themselves to be driven to clasping and colling and kissing and then he is on to her, panting, to pump in a thimbleload of seed. And in the devil's due time, which is three moons by three, a morris of Hecates, comes the child, and he grows and grows to hope from life, and then the smiting. It can be at any time. In my student days I saw children die at three days, and they were lucky, they had not grown to a day of hope. But I saw Tom die too, not twenty. And Chatterton died at seventeen. And here is the little poet Jack Keats dying at twenty-five, one of the luckier, for he has made bad poetry and seen something of the world. But it is the hope that is the curse, to be given hope and then hear the laughter."

"No curse, John. It is the second of the three great things, hope. Charity, which is the greatest, you have shown in abundance. It's only faith you lack. Hope that faith may come, hope for the sight of heaven."

"Severn," John said with calm quiet, "I will, I swear, gain enough strength to kill you if you spurt this sewage out at me. I have faith enough of my own, and it is faith in beauty that is eternal, so long as there are eyes to see it. I do not mean my own eyes, I have neither faith nor hope that these eyes will see a beauty not of the earth nor of the imagination. The earth and the heart and the imagination are all, and I am to have no more part in them. Oh, I may wake tomorrow and have hope that all will be well again, I feel better, I have appetite, the blood courses in its proper channels. But I do not wish more hope so that it may be cruelly quelled. Do you not understand me? There is neither virtue nor use in suffering. If the end is to come, let us have it, and not have the fiends of time at their game. But I will not ask again for a poor blessed twopenny engine of the end. I will lie here and see my body as nothing of mine. This hand I try to lift, see how cunningly fashioned, and it ploughdrove a pen once that scrawled bad hymns to beauty. But it is something now impertinently fastened to me and no longer anything of mine. I am something altogether apart from this machine. Yours, while this machine is to him. Shakespeare knew it all."

"Forgive me, John, do not be angry if I say you speak now more like a Christian. The soul, I mean. It is your soul you are thinking of now. Please, please, no anger, I say no more, but you must admit the truth of it."

"I do not mean that." John rolled his head feebly on the pillow. "Nor anything like that. For what you call my soul is the sparking of this machine. The brain too is the body. It is a fine and cunning trelliswork, but we may eat brain as we eat feet and flanks. But there is one thing that is not to be eaten and that is the little fire saying I am I am I am."

"That is God, that is the name God himself gave to Moses."

"And that little fire you have made there, no burning bush, that says it, and my fountain out there will say it long after this I is no more. So I will consign my own I elsewhere before it is wholly buried in this body that was named John Keats."

"John Keats is more than a body, as you know. Is not the imagination part of the soul? Forgive me again, I try not to speak too much like a Christian."

"It's all in decay, Severn. It was a clever machine, with the tongue and the teeth and the lips clacking and cooing most clever clusters of noises; and the noises long by common acceptance attached to things and thoughts and eager to be juggled in pretty poesy. But at the end there is only this I, shapeless and without memory or intelligence unless I consign it elsewhere. So for the moment I join it to the I of that singing water in the piazza and lose even my name. Or, if you will, write that name on water and hear the water gurgle on uncaring singing I, I, I."

"I wish I could understand you."

"Don't try, Severn. I'm not converting you to Keatsism— God forgive me and you forgive the empty formula, I-ism I would say. All of this machine is tired now, and the I, though never tired, must be courteous and lie quiet with it. I'll sleep back some blood." To Severn's surprise he sank instantly into sleep, and Severn thanked God. Then he tiptoed about the entire apartment, picking up razors, scissors, forks and table knives, and he locked all those death dealers in his trunk. But, he saw sadly, a man intent on his quietus could always find the bodkin: a sliver of windowpane, that firm lamphook there in the ceiling with the noose of his own bedsheet, the bodkin itself long mislaid by a long-dead seamstress. Severn went sadly to the black hole where the jakes was, then came back to John's bedroom to drink milk and gobble a hunk of yesterday's bread. As though he had awaited the return of his audience John started back to waking. He spoke quietly, saying: "Charles Jeremiah Wells is behind it."

"Wells? Wells behind what?" Severn choked on crust and coughed. John looked at him with calm eyes.

"Your cough is good and dry, Severn. It is not the fanfare heralding the princess in purple. I dreamed just now of that water outside, and there was a grinning man poisoning it. Wells poisoning wells. Did I not say I would poison him? He knew, you see, and now it is he does the poisoning. He is clever. All the way from London he sends his poison."

"John, you must not talk so. You know this is not possible."

"He was and is pure malignity. Why else should he hoax poor Tom with the dream of a foreign lady in love with him and drive poor Tom to desperation and death? I saw the letters he wrote about this lady. Tom dead of the phthisis, they said, but you and I know it was of a broken heart. But Wells will not let me too die of a broken heart. He began his poisoning before we left England. He contrives now to have the poisoning go on here in Rome. How is it done, all the way over the land and sea? He has his engines, Severn."

"You and I eat the same food. I am not poisoned."

"Ah no, he is above mere Renaissance subtleties. He is the Napoleonic poisoner and makes use of the telegraphic semaphore. You must exorcise with your Christian mumbo jumbo. But no, you have thrown out the devil, since gentle Jesus has not the Michelangelo muscles to fight him. He must not exist, the devil, and all must be pink froth of sweet goodness. Well, there are burly priests enow here and eke Latin. *Stabat mater dolorosa.* Their Christ here is the stiff standing prick, Signor Cristo Cazzuto. *Dum pendebat filius.*"

Severn was distressed. "John, we cannot have this. It is very unreasonable. Your mind is too busy. Let me read to you."

"What will you read—the Holy Bible? I approve the style but condemn the content. God's name, making man sinful so he could play with his hopes and terrors, has God nothing better to do? I figuratively cack on your Holy Bible, Severn." A bell started outside. "All gone already, the morning? Is that the Angelus?"

"It's too early for the Angelus. They toll the single bell."

"Well, not for me, not for the dirty Protestant. The filthy atheistical English poet. You know, Severn, when the time comes I must be buried at night? Belli told me that. Only the sons of the True Church may be earth-committed in daylight."

"You must not speak so, John. You must rest and be calm and get well again."

"Get Wells again. Isaac Marmaduke said he would kill Wells for me, but I think it will have been put out of his mind by other things. An unfairness about somewhere. Elton was to have done my dying for me." Then: "Severn, buy me laudanum."

"I said no, John, and must say it again. Please let us have no no no. More of this." Severn, to his own surprise, was weeping. John was sardonic-fatherly.

"Aye, aye, weep, dost thou, little one. Like Niobe. Well then, thou shalt be made laugh. Diddle diddle dumpling my son John beshat himself with's breeches on. It shan't happen, don't you see, Severn, it must not happen to this one. Can I not be preserved from that indignity?"

"You make me. I do not know what to. I wish I."

"Go paint the death of Socrates or some other bearded ancient, Severn. Be about your business, what you call your art. Or shall we have a symposium about my bed? Call them all in, Belli and hewing Ewing and Gulielmi, no he is with Shelley and his lordship in in where the tower leans, and our anglophilic Spaniard. But keep Clark in the dark, for he will be full of Calvinistic engines whose creaking jars. The Pope we could have if he would come, to see how a vile atheist dies."

"I will not have this," Severn, on his feet, his fists clenched with thumbs inside, cried, control lost. "I will not have this, do you hear?"

"Marry, because thou art atheistical dost thou think there shall be no more crusts and vinegar? You are right, Severn. I must look after you, I must not let you have *hysterica passio*."

"I will not have it, do you hear?"

"And I agree, do I not? Well, I will be calm." And then: "Wells, poisoning wicked Wells, the foul swine, you shall not prevail, there are engines to crush you and strong thumbs for the strangling."

Severn sobbed.

VII

"FOR US," CARDINAL FABIANI SAID, "THE FUTURE EXISTS."

"Yes, your eminence," said Belli. They had finished dinner—pasta with a rich meat sugo, Bracciano lake fish stuffed with sage and rosemary and roasted, roasted fowls, a winter salad, Sardinian cheese, eggs whipped with sugar and sherry, white and red wine, grappa and coffee—and sat before a log fire as wide as a stage in a chamber theatre. The salone of the villa on the Via Aurelia was full of holy and comfortably Italian art, but there were one or two pictures by the Spaniard who was really a Greek, containing placid whales into which crowds of people placidly proceeded. There were some Etruscan cups and vases filched from the tombs of Cerveteri, and there was some frank neopagan statuary by Canova. Cardinal Fabiani should have been fat but was thin, as if gnawed by an undying worm. He had vigorous ringed hands that flashed in the firelight. He poured more grappa for Belli. "Thank you, your eminence."

"We must not confuse the future with eternity. Eternity is not an endlessly prolonged future, it is a timeless state that wraps itself about time and, in odd places perceived chiefly by the holy, nibbles at it. Do you follow me?"

"Yes, your eminence. Very poetically put."

"However, to return to the future. In a few weeks 1821 commences. It will be a strange year. You know in what way or ways?"

"The death of Bonaparte, to begin with."

"Well, yes, the reports I have received, stemming ultimately from the Corsican physician Antommarchi, point to the completion of the task by early summer."

"The task? The completion?"

"The English are killing him under the guise of giving him the best medical treatment. Slow poisons, one presumes. However, however. He is to die, and he has time to die holily. He has murdered many by one means or another, and his purgatorial sojourn can hardly be brief. He has changed Europe," the Cardinal said sharply, as though making an epigram.

"One cannot doubt that, your eminence."

"And now Europe changes again. The Napoleonic flame flares, as if sugar had been thrown on it, for one last time, and the big grandiloquent odes will be written."

"Not by me, your eminence."

"Not by you, my son. What is this I hear about your losing your taste for grandiloquence? There is a sonnet of yours going about, one written in the Roman dialect. It condemns or scorns or something some holy poem written on the Blessed Virgin."

"I do not condemn the substance but the form. There are some self-styled poets in the Academy of the Tiber who launch words like balloons. I prefer my words to be small but full of gravity. Mass, not size. Napoleon's death will launch plenty of balloons, your eminence. They will all come down. Now a word of metal makes no pretension to flying."

"You are not here, my son, to deliver a theory of literature."

"No, your eminence. You started it, with respect, your eminence."

"You are here," kindly smiling, up on his feet, ringed fist banging Belli's shoulder, "to discuss the future of Rome and your future in the Rome of the future."

"How far into the future, your eminence?"

The cardinal prepared to kick back a log dislodging, saw that he had a silk slipper on, desisted. Belli thrust out his booted foot without otherwise stirring from his chair and smartly sent the log back in a grumble of sparks to nest again with its fellows.

"Well, now, we gained our independence from the French Empire six years back. His Holiness resumed rule of a city that had tasted the rank meat of Jacobin republicanism—"

"*Rank,* I question that *rank* with respect. Fresh meat rather, very bloody. *Rank* suggests long-hung and mouldy."

"Like," the quick prelate said, "the city itself. You were about to say that, were you not?"

"No, but since you have put the idea into my head, your eminence, I will now say, with respect and in the humility of a son of Rome, yes. Yes. Our drains are bad, our streets carry no name plaques, we lack light—"

"So the *Urbs Lucis* lacks light, does it?"

"I am talking of the physical city, your eminence. In London they now have gas lighting, so a London visitor told me."

Cardinal Fabiani shook two gemmed fingers brilliantly at Belli. "I know very well what you are talking about, and my response then was by way of a rebuke. You are slow sometimes, my son. What does the physical city matter? This is the City of God, and all above the dirt and madness of the body."

"The Holy Father is a temporal ruler. There are, with respect, such things as temporal obligations."

"We have no ambition here to be London or St Petersburg—"

"We are already St Petersburg, we were re-founded as St P—"

"Very sillily clever, you are always ready with your word play and your word play may well prove your undoing, my son. You are not here drinking my wine and eating my victuals to indulge in your silly games of the Academy of the Tiber. You are here to consider the future of Rome."

"I'm flattered, your eminence, that I should be considered worthy."

"Giuseppe Gioacchino, you are no fool, otherwise I would not put up as I do with your nonsense. No fool, but no thinker either. It is your flashes I want, what I suppose you would call your imagination."

"The vatic, the poet as *vates*. Thus flash I forward to the future, eminence. His Holiness will not rule this city for ever. The papacy as military power, which is all civil power has ever meant on this peninsula—the notion was already dying with Julius II. And that one dying on St Helena, he is thought to have lost but has really won. He has taught the new idea of the unified nation, and the idea will not be long in coming here."

"Bonaparte was never an idea, he was a man, my son, mortal but endowed with a devilish big ability. Such men are not ten a penny. He ate the papacy for breakfast, but it will be centuries before such another comes. Peter's seat is safe."

"Yes, eminence, if by Peter you mean merely the keeper of the keys."

"Merely? *Merely?*" But Cardinal Fabiani poured Belli more grappa.

"I prophesy that the secular rule of the papacy will be over in, oh, say twenty years. His Holiness, whoever it shall be, must keep within his Vatican walls and smirk at the Roman populace from St Peter's at Christmas and Easter. From a balcony, very high up. The secular power will be in hands as yet unknown and the Pope will be reviled and sneered at as a ruler of Christian souls, for the soul itself will be sneered at as a pretentious silly hypothesis. The kingdoms of Italy will be made into one kingdom and Rome has as good a chance as Milan or Turin of being its capital city. Better, perhaps, because of its position."

"Kingdom, you say. Who will be king?"

"Whoever the kingmaker decides on. And do not ask me to name the kingmaker because he may be now a snotty boy peeing his breeches. I apologise, your eminence."

"You have this Roman coarseness in you, my son. So that is your picture of the Roman future, eh?"

"Not a future I greatly relish. I'm temperamentally incapable of thinking in terms of—big national unities. Italy to me is the name of a land leg and a land belly above belted with spiky mountains. I'm a Roman and it's enough to be a Roman. What's good enough for a Caesar is good enough for a Belli. Soon they'll be talking of a language called Italian which any good Italian patriot must speak and write, forgetting his Roman, and his Venetian or Milanese for that matter, disregarded dialects with literatures ignored by the big *dottori*. Bad as things are here and now, I prefer them to what's to come."

"Bad?"

"Oh, what I said—the stink of uncollected garbage, robbers in alleys, no street lamps, too many jacks-in-office."

"Of whom you are one."

"A very small jack, your eminence. Just big enough to stop me living off my wife."

"You could," Cardinal Fabiani said, "be a *very* big one." Belli said nothing. He looked into the golden firecave, waiting. "I reject your prophecy," his eminence said. Belli shrugged

Romanly. "Things will not be as you say, at least not in our lifetime."

"You must, as ever speak for yourself, eminence."

The prelate ignored that. "Expect hotheads, a renewal of jacobinism, republican claptrap, inept pasquinades, inflammatory pamphlets, street-corner evocations of a Bonaparte who ceased to exist even before the turn of the century. Rome, however, will not yield one whit of its ancient and blessedly recovered divine authority. What do you say, my son, to a central bureau of censorship of which you shall be the head?"

"Censorship? More than already exists?"

"The theatres as well as the newspapers. The opera house. Poems and novels and cheapjack modernist metaphysics. The printed and spoken and enacted word. What do you say?"

Belli got up to kick back into confirmation of its place a log that had been proposing dislodgement for half an hour past. He remained standing, looking down on the meagre prelate who by *our lifetime* could mean no more than a meagre decade. He said: "There will be more police too, paid for with a heavier tax on salt and tobacco. With respect, your eminence, always with respect, I wonder how far you, a man of the Campagna, understand the Roman mind. Wait, with respect, and let me say my word, since it was for my word you asked me here to eat your fish and pullets. You can do anything to a Roman—indeed, you *must* do anything to a Roman, touching the very limit of oppression. A Roman expects nothing from his rulers except tyranny of one sort or another. Treat a Roman well and he will begin to think there is a catch somewhere and start brooding revolution. Probably they deserve to be so treated, the rats of this foul and beautiful sewer. They are probably all damned, and hell is a city much like Rome. They have no notion of morality, none of theology, none at all of history. Ignorant and damned. To many Romans Rome is a tract only in space and not at all in time, so that the tyrannous Popes and Caesars share a kind of mythic contemporaneity. For that matter, Cain murdered Abel in an alley off the Piazza Navona, and Noah modelled his ark on the Porto de Ripetta ferry. That a bird impregnated our Blessed Mother none find it difficult to believe, since after all *bird* is another name for *prick*—"

"You are getting off your point, whatever your point is or was."

"The Roman tongue has more words for *prick* and *balls* and *cunt* than any language in the world. They believe in nothing but hardship and getting drunk and fucking. Oh, they accept Christian doctrine as they accept Romulus and Remus and the mother-wolf, and they think that Pontius Pilate delivered his judgment in St Peter's. It seems very reasonable to them that God should play a dirty trick with an apple and then say: *Posterity, you're fucked.* They are all fucked and in turn they fuck. What I suppose I am saying is this, your eminence—for God's sake, with respect, don't dream of a holy city which can be made even holier by cutting off the outside world from its denizens. They don't believe the outside world exists, most of them—"

"You speak," said Cardinal Fabiani, at last sitting down on a chair whose arms writhed with cherubim, "of the common people, and you, my son, have used very common language in speaking of them."

"*Mea maxima culpa.* Holiness in others brings out the worst in myself. I am a positive saint in the company of atheistical sneerers. Common people? A holy city surely talks of souls all equal in God's eyes. Anyway, even poets and intellectuals Roman-born have enough of the common Roman inside them. I myself have. I try to keep it down, not always with success, then I yield and beat my breast after. The language which is my language, and which Dante's Tuscan disdains, is made out of melons and flyblown meat and piss and shit and—"

"I think we have had enough of that, my son."

"Yes, your eminence, I see we have. I am not good at censoring my own mind. I wonder you should so wish to honour me by—this proposal."

Cardinal Fabiani said nothing. He sat, hands folded, chewing crossly at some remnant of dinner that a hollow tooth had coyly cached and now yielded. "Do you think of God ever?" he asked at last. "Of the nature of God, of God's ultimate quiddity?"

Belli sat. "That, surely, is all laid down. The Church in its infinite wisdom instructs us as to the nature of divinity. As a Roman, of course, I have a somewhat undivine and non-eternal image of the eternal divine. What, may I ask, respect, respect and always respect, has this to do with censorship?"

"Everything," fiercely. "Everything. The terrible purity of God," more fiercely, "is what it is all about. Do you meditate ever on this terrible terrible purity?"

Belli nodded seriously and then thought for a minute before giving a verbal answer. "I have a clear enough image of God," he said, "but it is my own and perhaps heretical, perhaps too paganly platonic to be acceptable to my spiritual betters."

"Beware of Plato, my son. Aristotle is our rock."

"I think of a sonnet," Belli said.

"Mad, mad, are you mad?"

"Wait. Eminence. Respect, etcetera. The sonnet form must have existed *in potentia* from the beginning, but it was made flesh with such as Petrarch. Behind the thousands of sonnets in the world, in Tuscan, Roman, French, German, even English, shines the one ultimate perfect sonnet. It has fourteen lines that divide into an octave of a rhyme scheme ABBA ABBA and a sestet CDC DCD, really two tercets. One may vary the rhymes a little but the essential shape will remain. The wordless sonnet that still rhymes, that says nothing, having no words, but yet speaks. It says: I am this, but I am also this. In my eight lines X, in my six lines Y, but in my total fourteen ever the unity, the ultimate statement whose meaning its itself. What is this, your eminence, but the true image of God?"

"Heretical, yes, you were right when you said that. You talk of an abstraction, a ghost."

"I talk of an ultimate reality. And through the glimmering of it I have given you, a soul may speak to a soul. A Roman writes a sonnet on the divine beauty, and an Englishman writes a sonnet on an old tomcat, and neither understands the other's language, but in the recognition of the common form they meet." Shame suddenly washed him all over, like a sweat premonitory of crapulous vomiting. What devil made him do that, to tear up rudely a sick Englishman's homage? So, devil, was it? He would go and apologise, if he could find where he lived. Gulielmi knew, but Gulielmi had gone away. But tomorrow he might not feel like making apologies. It was, after all, a ribald and unworthy effusion wagging a beshitten tail. He had been right to suppress it, wrong to trust Gulielmi with it a whole day before its suppression. And yet the form in the mind of God did not reject it, any more than God himself rejected *cazzi* and *fiche* and the other dirty commodities of his creation. He might yet apologise, but it might be difficult to find out where the sick English poet lived. Or was dying. Cardinal Fabiani was saying something.

"—has always acknowledged, in its God-given wisdom, man's lower nature. The confessional is ever open for the discharge of the shameful ordures of humanity. But men must not wallow, they must be led, nay forced, to identification with their higher selves. Or, if you wish that in political terms, repressive government and occasional carnivals. Will you become our censor, in the service of a repression that is itself in the service of God's plan for the humanity he made in his own image and likeness?"

"Give me time to think of it. Time to come to terms with my own unworthiness."

VIII

⌒

"So, Severn, she said 'Voulez-vous profiter de ma caresse, *monsieur?*' and I, nothing loth, sneered up at the liveried tiger who sneered down, passing beneath him on my quick passage to the other door of her coach, and I was in there breathing the richness of her perfume, which was roses and violets and Eastern spices, Severn, and we galloped through the dirty streets not to the Villa Borghese but to the palazzo to which her husband the prince has banished her, Severn. He has banished her because she is too ready to summon any pretty man to her bed. Well, now it was I who was summoned and I was nothing loth. How shall I describe to you that long night caressing her long nakedness, holding in my arms the princess of love who is the sister of him who was like to be emperor of all the world? No prodigal outpouring of poesy's most opulent treasure could convey one whit of the ecstasies spent freely and as freely renewed.

"The bed itself, Severn, was in form of a gold trireme and the coverlet was of silk containing the down of innumerable eiderducks and cygnets. The sheets too were of silk that gave off crackles of electricity when we crawled thereon naked towards each other from opposed angles. She instructed me in all of the modes of physical possession out of her deep learning. Marry, I cannot remember the names of them all, but there was certes the pavonian touch, the Ledan straddle too, the chthonian ditch, the I think it was termed Ceutan flight and eke the Madrilenan interuberal. When, sweating and briefly weary of our sport, she rang for refreshment, the wine we drank we drank from heavy bronze cups with dove-feet, and there was fruit with, though this must seem impossible, dawn dew upon it though midnight had scarce struck. All this I tell you is true, Severn, in poetic truth it is all true.

"Guilt? Why should guilt touch me with its scaly wing? I have been faithful to the limit, have I not? Would it be just for me to be denied what his lordship takes with such aristocratic carelessness daily, nightly, matutinally, postmeridianly, serally? She should have yielded when I asked, Severn, but I well remember the afternoon when, her mother gone out visiting, we stood looking at each other's feet, unwilling to engage each other's eyes, our breasts heaving, and she said somewhat to the effect that this was the fate imposed upon us by a social order that chains neither the milord nor the stinking swinking I would say artisan but reserves its bondage for all who wear clean shirts and pressed muslin and chat with the rector after matins but have nothing in goldsmith's notes. Ah, the risk and the scandal. But I, Severn, have had a whole manhood of fleshly longing crammed into a boy's years, and Alma Venus or Queen Mab or *l'ultima principessa* could give in no wise to my fancy what she she she denied to my body.

"Then thousand curses and stinging blights light on it all and on her too who turned her desirable back on the prospect of a paradise pardieu for herself as much as for me, poor dogsbody, Severn. I wanted her so much, stripped of her demure muslin and her warm body snaking or lamiating in my warm arms, hers and hers only and to the inferno with Alma Venus. God or whoever's up there rain down stinking ordures on her who withheld so through fear of Mr Snigg and Mistress Sniff and the Reverend Snoggsbody and invoked an unjust propriety

to leave me quenching my fire with cold water and tired let-
tuce leaves. Radishes and onions and eke turnips and potatoes
are, e'en uncompanioned with gross bloody beef or fat lusty
pork, promoters enow of lawless lechery. And Burton laughed,
I swear his laugh broke an instant from the frontispiece wood-
cut of his wry costive countenance.

"Well, he was in the right of it, e'en so your worship. And
all the poets dead and gone laughed too and laugh still. This
afternoon I had a long colloquy with mad Will, who speaketh
good Florentine I may say, though he was helped out on a
word here and there by Master Florio, ever banging at his
open dictionary as at the King's Bible. But in fair English
he told me, the sounds sweetly Italianate, and after a while he
laughed but little, that there is nothing after this, neither fire
nor ice, for he has wandered like a ghost and longed to lap
blood. There is nothing, saith he, like the red din of an aching
tooth as it engageth good hot meat, nor the nutmeg and cinnamon in mulled ale thudding on the arch of the palate, nor
the dove-soft touch of a young love's ripening breast.

"Of that I could endite well, Severn. Had I but had time
and sense I could have writ a great long poem on the sweetness
of the breasts of the enchantresses of history, from Helen to
Alma Venus here in Rome who has had her right breast modelled in marble by Maestro Canova or some such rogue. And
of the aching sweetness of the soft swell outwards from the
waist to the buttocks, and the faint sweet down on the skin.
Away with your bloodless Jesus, I say.

"Well, no, not so truly, since he had blood enough in him
and fire enough and his whipping arm was strong. It is that the
enemy of the world has filched and perverted him, the enemy
that rules now, Severn, and you would wish to know who he

is and behold I will tell thee. He is all against life, meaning the thud of the heart in venery, the savour of claret, the clamorous morsels of spring in the nest you by chance uncover, hawthorn and goldenrod, good witty lechery in the company of men, the green waving tree, tough-boled, of the body. It is not enough for him to suck blood only at once to spew it forth, he must also poison the very wells of blood. His name may be Wells for all we know, or Flibbertigibbet or Cacasona, it matters not. He is cacodemon of decay, and it is not the decay of the grass-dropped apple in autumn. For the apple dies in sweetness but I do not.

"I do not, Severn, I do not not not. Nor do I proceed to the consummation with speed enow. You see, I do not curse the brevity of this my allotment, for your three score and ten superstition puts silly value on the straight line of the geometers, which has length but not thickness. I have had thickness enough, God knows, and now I am hawking up the thickness—blood less and less, a rank porridge more and more. I regret only that I was denied the one sweetness Lord Byron would have crushed carelessly between his fine teeth, like a horse grinding a sugar lump. He would have taken her if he could and then confounded the memory of her caresses with a myriad others, not even remembering her name—*Fanny something, but there have been so many Fanny somethings.* So my craving was not inordinate, Severn, and it was denied.

"I reserve a special curse for Society, which has as ultimate head of its Executive the Life Hater. Ah, how Society feels itself threatened by the human senses! Even the chomp and honey drip of language, made of sense and bound to sense as it is, must be squeezed dry by Society. And yet I, disregarded small poet, am one of the sustainers of Society and, in a sense, must die for it. When will it be, Severn, the end? I curse you again and I curse Clark for withholding the drowsy quietus. Curse you and your fucking nasty perverted gentle Jesus whining about the sanctity of life. Curse every follicle, each footsole's grimy whorl, each inbreath and eke each outbreath, muddy Severn, torturer. I will haunt your grey age, enemy."

Severn heard none of this.

Severn heard Dr Clark's words with buzzing ears, squinting at him with aching eyes in the cool sunlit afternoon at the foot of the Spanish Steps. It was almost Christmas and Abruzzese bagpipes droned and wailed on the light wind.

"You look near dead, man." Clark spoke English with a Scotch tune. "You cannot put up much longer with this waking and watching. You'll be screaming soon, screaming at a screamer. I must bring a nurse in."

"We have not the money."

"Never mind about the money. You can, I'm sure, get more money from the men who brought out his poems. Did not those poems just lately go into another edition?"

"That was John's joke, God help him. He said for me to write to Taylor there would be a second printing. *In cold sheets* were his words. It is his grave humour you must call it. I see no prospect of money. Dying is as expensive as living."

The physician Clark had summoned for a second opinion was further up the Steps, talking to Don Benedetto of the church up there. He was a Roman believed by some to have the evil eye and named only by his initials, M.P.

"What are they talking of?" Severn said fretfully. "I don't like this hand-waving and shrugging and pointing back at the house. John raves and screams, true, but he cannot help it. I suppose they will have it there's a devil in him." He muttered: "So there is, God forgive me for saying it."

"Passing the time of day, no more," Clark soothed. "You must take small notice of these Roman gestures." And then: "He's a good doctor, so good that they think there's witchcraft in him, some. He confirmed my diagnosis and prognosis. And the treatment too. So you're not to worry any more about that."

"The starvation is to go on? And the blood letting?"

"It's only the way, laddie. It's the coughing up of the blood that kills him with the weakness. He must take no more blood in. The diet of steamed fish is the right one. And not too much of that either."

"He's ceased giving out blood, you know that."

"There you are, then."

"He casts up some thick grey substance. Keats's porridge he terms it. More of his murky humour."

"He's a noble animal, God help him."

"Is there no more you can do than bleeding and starving?"

"Ask the man up there if there's more. He's seen consumption enough in his time. Half the town has it."

"So we bring our English consumptives to a town where half have it. I see."

"Come now, Rome's climate often has a fine effect on northern sufferers. John Keats's life will go on longer than it would have in Hampstead. I wager we'll prolong it to the spring."

"For what purpose? For what purpose do you prolong it?"

"Come now, Severn, you must not ask that question. That's the atheistical question that our poor friend asks. Don't let him infect you."

"I'm close to him all day and all night too," Severn said in a high strained voice. "It's hard to avoid that risk."

"Pull yourself together, man. I'll get that nurse tomorrow."

"Oh, I've help enough. Ewing comes and the Spaniard Llanos. The English chaplain too, but John will not have him. He persists in cursing the Christian faith." Severn began to snivel.

"Aye, well, you must keep yourself strong for that duty. You must not let him go out an atheist with his blather about the creative imagination and the rest of the poetic godlessness. God forgive me for saying that. He's a better man than most of the Christians I know. But our view of him isn't necessarily the Almighty's."

Severn went back in to a quieted emaciated John with eyes like lamps. The voice was not the voice Severn had known even a month back. It was higher and sharper, like an old man's, the Cockney vowels more pronounced, the tones too often those of malignity. "So, Severn, they've confirmed that I'm dying in my stomach, yes? The lungs are pink and spongy and bursting with healthful air. And I'm to go on being starved, yes? Listen. Severn, I ask you no more to buy me laudanum, but I do ask that you bring me in a beefsteak, cold maybe but well-cooked. See, my mouth oozes for a beefsteak."

"You know I cannot, you know it will only bring the blood. I must obey the—"

"Always obey, Severn, and you will get on in the world. Obey the dictates of Society and Medicine and the Edinburgh Arbiters of Art and you will be a baronet some day. Very well, read me something."

"Jeremy Taylor? *Holy Living and Holy Dying?*"

"I like it for the wrong reasons, you know that, Severn."

"How do you know it is for the wrong reasons? I think perhaps you like to convince yourself that the spirit is not at last working on you. But I see differently."

"Bugger the spirit, Severn. Read."

Severn read: "'There is no state, no accident, no circumstance of our life, but it hath been soured by some sad instance of a dying friend: a friendly meeting often ends in some sad mischance, and makes an eternal parting: and when the poet Aeschylus was sitting under the walls of his house, an eagle hovering over his bald head mistook it for a stone, and let fall his oyster, hoping there to break the shell, but pierced the poor man's skull.'"

John laughed. "I had always thought it was a tortoise the eagle dropped, but still— You see what I mean, Severn, about the wrong reasons. Taylor is lively, there is no gloom of death in him. Read on."

"'Death meets us everywhere, and is procured by every instrument and in all chances, and enters in at many doors; by violence and secret influence, by the aspect of a star and the stink of a mist, by the emissions of a cloud and the meeting of a vapour, by the fall of a chariot and the stumbling at a stone, by a full meal or an empty stomach—'"

"That bites hard, Severn, very hard."

"'—By watching at the wine or by watching at prayers, by the sun or the moon, by a heat or a cold, by sleepless nights or sleeping days, by water frozen into the hardness and sharpness of a dagger, or water thawed in the floods of a river, by a hair or a raisin, by violent motion or sitting still, by severity or dissolution, by God's mercy or God's anger; by everything in providence and everything in manners, by everything in nature and everything in chance—'"

"He takes such pleasure in his doublets. Hair or raisin, indeed. There's no death in it at all."

" '—*Eripitur persona, manet res;* we take pains to heap up things useful to our life, and get our death in the purchase; and the person is snatched away, and the goods remain. And all this is the law and constitution of nature; it is a punishment of our sins, the unalterable event of providence, and the decree of heaven: the chains that confine us to this condition are strong as destiny, and immutable as the eternal laws of God.' " Severn looked up. "May I stop there? I can hardly keep my eyes open."

"Sleep then. I shall not leap out of bed to buy beefsteaks or laudanum." And then: "Poor Severn. Poor Joseph. Did they call you Joe at home?" Severn nodded and the nod turned to a nodding off which he jerked himself out of abruptly when John said: "Sometimes in the night's deep watches I anagrammatise my name, give its constituent letters to such things of the world to survive as will take them. Keats takes steak. Alas, he does not. Stake takes Keats. A different stake, for martyr's burning. John Keats thanks Joe. And so the name is pulled apart and there is an end to it. Have you made arrangements for my Protestant burial yet?"

"I would—I have—"

"Sleep, sleep, Joe. Ah, alas, you cannot yet." For there was a knocking at the door of the apartment. Severn tottered from John's bedroom to open up to Signora Angeletti, very voluble with much hand work, and two stolider persons, men in stained blue uniform. Severn could not well understand what was being said. These were officials of some sort, sent by whom? Signora Angeletti babbled on about *la legge, la legge.* "Bring them in to me," called John.

They stood then at the bed's foot. One of the men, smelling death, made a sign of the cross with great speed. Signora Angeletti spoke on and on, apologetic, bold, sympathetic, asserting her rights.

"What is it?" Severn said. "What in God's name—"

"Wait." And John heard her out and heard what she said confirmed more briefly in the Roman basso of the elder of the two men. "It's the law, Severn. Everything is to be burnt at the stake—furniture, books, the very wallpaper. I am a source of infection to the city. I am to be allowed to die first, but then comes the burning."

"It's that man Clark brought, it's that damnable priest at the top of the Steps—"

"It's the law, Severn. *La legge, capisco,*" he said to Signora Angeletti and the two men. They all nodded, thankful to be understood. Nothing personal, they would that the signore could live and flourish, but as he was dying and they had it on medical authority confirmed by the Church that he was then there was nothing for it but the burning and they were sincerely sorry about the expense. "We have to find the money, Severn. To replace what is to be burnt. *La legge,* you understand. I'm truly sorry, truly. I take back what I said about wishing to die quickly. I must die slowly and grant you time to raise the money." Severn raised pathetic fists towards his temples and was ready to scream. "Calm, calm. There will be time, I promise you. I will expire slowly, like a good boy."

IX

JOHN KEATS'S NIGHTLY MUSIC WAS FROM A TINY FOUNTAIN
in the shape of a boat; Belli's was the torrent of Trevi, which
he lived above. He and his wife had an apartment in the Poli
palazzo, whose windows, like the eyes of the sculpted figures
that preside over the waters, looked straight on to the pool
and the jets that thrashed into it. Belli was in his study with
Gulielmi a week after Epiphany, both standing, both looking
down absently into the foam rainbowed by the bright noon.
Gulielmi was just back from the north. He had announced
that Carlo Porta was dead. He had died of gout the day before
Epiphany.

"I should have gone to Milan to see him," Belli said. "He
was a great poet."

"A great *dialect* poet."

"Dialect, dialect, dialect. What in God's name is the difference between a language and a dialect? I'll tell you. A language
waves flags and is blown up by politicians. A dialect keeps to
things, things, things, street smells and street noises, life."

"Well, now your way is clear. You must replace Porta. No,
don't burst out again. As the great poet of dialect. Yes, I know,
comparing Milanese and Roman is like comparing French and
Spanish, but I mean what you mean—things, appetites, feel-
ings, odours, people, not the big bannered abstractions."

"I've thought of this," Belli said. "Thought of it especially
since the great man offered me the great position. Belli on the
side of the State, gelder of thought and speech in the service

of stability. Belli at nightfall, saving his reason through scurrility. All literature is subversive, somebody said. Voltaire? A repressive office will force me into a métier of subversion. I acknowledge myself to be a split man."

"We're all split. Meat is disgusting, some Englishman said, but it's also delicious. The act of love is bestial but also ecstatic."

"Stability saved through scurrility. Subversion the prop of social order."

"It's the literature that counts. You embrace a kind of martyrdom to write what you have to write. Have you considered what you have to write?"

"Stuff for tavern recitation with the doors closed. Totally unpublishable."

"But what?"

"Time, time, I must be given time. I'm not ready."

The furnishings of the study expressed the contradictions in the man—a plain deal kitchen table, a tavern chair and a chair of French provenance, very fine, an old prie-dieu with stuffed satin well knee-worn, a lectern with an open Jerome, a Jacobin etching showing a generic pope as a feeder of children to a greybeard cannibal God, Lotto's Annunciation (a bad copy) with its cat running scared from Gabriel. On the table was John Keats's cat sonnet, with a literal translation by Gulielmi.

"That boy there," Gulielmi said, "spoke to me of a great long poem about Rome—changing Rome and the unchanging Roman. My heart ached with pity when he told me. I knew it was not for him."

"Changing Rome, indeed. Rome doesn't change, Rome must not be viewed temporally. No work for an outsider. But he's on the right lines in another way. I'm sorry I sneered at this cat sonnet of his."

"Whatever you do, Belli, for God's sake don't take that poem as typical. He's not that kind of poet at all. He's a poet of nature, romance, fairyland, heartache, the classical world as seen in a rainy English garden. That cat sonnet's a mere joke."

"Joke or not, he's on the right lines there. The sonnet form can be dragged low, must be dragged low. The time has come to reject its Petrarchal coronation. You see, God is in cabbage patches and beer-stains on a tavern table. Do you follow me?"

"No."

"I was so bitterly ashamed of that *cazzo* sonnet—you remember it?"

"Can I ever forget?"

"One must trust one's instinct more. I was really proclaiming the glory of God. Do you follow me?"

"No."

"Never mind. I have some Madeira here. A present from— Never mind. Do you like Madeira?"

"With a biscuit. Do you have a biscuit?"

Belli opened his battered escritoire and disclosed bits of old food—cheese, stale bread, a hunk of salami tough as pemmican. "I sometimes," he said apologetically, "need a little something when working late. Here are *English* biscuits. That Spanish fellow gave them to me. Planos?"

"Llanos. Hm, still eatable." Belli poured sweet golden wine. "Hm, not bad really."

"Perhaps," Belli said, having sipped, "I should not say *the glory of God*. Perhaps, as ever, I go too far." Gulielmi waited, having expected this. "You see, I will end with some— You see, only the other day I heard a Roman workman saying how much he hated work. He said it was hypocritical of priests, who do nothing anyway, extolling the virtues of toil, when the final virtue is to do nothing. In heaven, this man said, the male saints do nothing all day except play with their balls while the female saints merely scratch their cunts." Gulielmi laughed until he choked on biscuit crumbs. Belli remained grave. "I see that," he said, "as a perfect sonnet. I even heard the rhymes lining themselves up. It *has* to be set down, aromatic Roman speech haloed by a sonnet. How can I talk about doing it to the glory of God?" He seemed genuinely distressed.

"The glory of man," Gulielmi said, after coughing. "But never mind. And now let me tell you what your task is. This boy Keats—whom I must go to visit, and soon, before it is too late—Keats, I say, dreamed that his big Roman poem could be all in sonnets. He was, even if he were to live, the wrong man for it. The work is reserved to you. You depict unchanging Rome through its many voices. You write two thousand, three thousand sonnets. All about dirty cynical suffering rejoicing Rome, and all in Roman voices. Not your voice, not that. *Their* voices. Why should that make you feel guilty?"

"I'm tempted," Belli said. "Sorely tempted, God help me." He raised his fist to his breast as though to beat it, then opened his fist to grasp his Madeira glass. He sketched, before drinking, a shy gesture of toasting the project.

X

"I HAVE CONVERSED WITH SOME MEN WHO REJOICED IN THE death or calamity of others, and accounted it as a judgment upon them for being on the other side, and against them in the contention: but within the revolution of a few months, the same man met with a more uneasy and unhandsome death: which, when I saw, I wept, and was afraid; for I knew that it must be so with all men; for we also shall die, and end our quarrels and contentions by passing to a final sentence."

He read no more Jeremy Taylor. He read no more of anything. Wells and the *Edinburgh Review* would be judged in God's good time, whoever or whatever God was. He was to die without the consolation granted to the horniest-handed ploughman. He was content. It was enough to be born to the morning sun and the morning milk and account this waking a sort of triumph.

He was too weary to try to separate out the imagined, the dreamt and the quotidian real. Breathing became a craft to be practised with painful attention. If he slept the craft might be removed from him.

Many stood or sat by his bed. Llanos said he would go to England and speak to those left. Gulielmi said that Belli could not visit him, having now much on his mind, but he apologised for his brutal want of courtesy that evening so far back and wished to express admiration for such of a fellow-poet's work as he could, with Gulielmi's help, be brought to understand. The Princess Borghese, Pauline Bonaparte, came looking for the handsome Elton. Elton himself obligingly appeared, on his way to Switzerland, and coupled with her on John's bed, John obligingly tucking his feet up to make room. His own dear girl came in black and said that mourning altogether forbade even the most mildly wanton loveplay.

So that was acceptable and all was, in a word, well.

He had one dream or vision that shocked him at first with a sense of blasphemy, though it must be a sense borrowed from Severn, since he who did not believe could not well blaspheme. Christ *pendebat* from his cross and cried ABBA ABBA. Now John knew that this was the Aramaic for father father, but he knew better that it was the rhyme scheme of a Petrarchan sonnet octave. It came to him thus that the sonnet form might subsist above language, but he did not see how this was possible. Language itself was perhaps only a ghost of the things in the outer world to which it adhered, and a ghost of a ghost was a notion untenable totally. And yet it seemed that two men, of language mutually unintelligible, might in a sense achieve communication through recognition of what a sonnet was. Belli and himself, for instance. Then breathing became a craft to be craftily learnt again, a matter of catching the gods of unbreathing off their guard.

St Valentine's Day came, and with it Valentino Llanos to announce he would go to England soon. Then a week passed and two more days, and John knew his dying day had come, yet to achieve death might be a day's hard labour. Severn held him, as it were carrying him to the gate, but he could not bear Severn's laboured breathing, for it struck like ice. To put off the world outside—the children's cries, snatches of song, a cheeping spar-row, the walls and the wallpaper and the chairs that thought they would outlast him but would not, the sunlight streaking the door—was not over-difficult. A bigger problem was to separate himself from his body—the hand worn to nothing, the lock of hair that fell into his eye, even the brain that scurried with thoughts and words and images. It took long hours to die.

"I'm. Sorry. Severn. My weight."

"Nothing, it's nothing, rest now."

He tried to give up breathing, to yield to the breathless gods, but his body, worn out as it was, would not have that. It pumped in its feeble eggspoons of Roman air, motes in the sun and all, but there seemed to be nothing in his body to engage the air. The afternoon wore on to evening and his brain was fuddled and he groped for the essence he had called I. It fell through his fingers.

"John. John."

There was nothing there to make any answer. Severn dropped the body to the bed and the body gave out some teaspoons of fluid and a final sigh.

The quiet house became busy. The apartment was stripped of everything, and the children gaped at the carts outside in the piazza, on to which furniture, rugs, rolls of stripped off wallpaper were piled, to be taken off for the burning. Signora Angeletti presented a bill. "I have money enough, fear not, madam," Severn said. "Only enough, but enough." The plates and cups they had used, these he smashed with his cane, smashed and smashed while Signora Angeletti cried, *"Accidenti."*

The body was opened up by Drs. Clark and M.P. There were no lungs left. There were no lungs left at all. The lungless body was placed in a plain deal coffin and the lid hammered on by undertaker's men who coughed from the fumigation. A plot had been reserved in the Protestant Cemetery.

Belli came reluctantly, almost dragged by Gulielmi, to the Piazza di Spagna before dawn. The mourners felt the February chill, their breath visible in the lamps of the hearse and the carriages. The coffin was taken down the stairs and appeared at the door when Don Benedetto arrived on the square, ready to climb the Steps for early service. He nodded at Gulielmi and Belli. He knew them both.

"A very young man," he said. "A poet, was he not?"

"An English poet," Belli said. "Now dead of consumption."

"We know not the day nor the hour," said Don Benedetto, who was fat, hale, nearly sixty. "These Protestants," he added.

"He did not call himself a Protestant," Gulielmi said. "He was a saintly young man, but he was neither Protestant nor Catholic."

Don Benedetto puffed at that *saintly.* "Interred in the dark," he said. "Darkness to darkness."

"What," said Belli, "do you mean by that?"

"The unenlightened. We may not even speak of invincible ignorance. All those nations that have turned their backs on the light."

"He had," Belli said, "more light in his little toe than you have in your entire fat carcase."

"No," said Gulielmi. "Please. Not now."

"I know nothing of him," Belli said, "but that I am prepared to say again and again. Priests live by the letter and poets by the word. Do you not say anything about poets turning their backs to the light."

"You are understandably upset," the priest said, "and it is early and chilly and dark. I will pretend I did not hear what you said."

"Oh, I said it," Belli cried. "Wipe that sanctimonious smirk from your jowls or I will wipe it for you."

"Please," Gulielmi said.

"Bloodsuckers, preyers on the people, purveyors of gloom, fear and uncharity."

"You will hear more of this," Don Benedetto said. He began to climb the Steps.

"*You* will hear more, you mean," Belli cried after him. "Much more, bloated parasite." And then, to Gulielmi: "God forgive me, what gets into me?"

The cortège was ready to move off.

PART TWO

So John Keats died on February 23, 1821, and Napoleon Bonaparte died a little over two months later. Percy Bysshe Shelley, having presented Keats in *Adonais* as a sensitive plant choked by weeds but paradoxically surviving his killers in the form of a spirit of Eternal Beauty, was drowned in 1822, reduced to ashes on an heroic pyre, then, like Keats, interred in the Protestant Cemetery of Rome. Lord Byron, fighting for the independence of Greece, died in Greece in 1824. The intensest phase of the Romantic Movement was thus coming to an end.

Lieutenant Elton died in Switzerland a year and more after the death of Keats. Joseph Severn returned to England but went back to Rome, there to live long as British consul and to become a venerable Roman figure. Valentino Llanos visited England, met Fanny Brawne and Fanny Keats, John's sister, married the latter and took her to Spain when the political atmosphere there had grown more liberal. They lived happily. Dr Clark became physician to Queen Victoria and was knighted. Belli became a censor and wrote 2,279 sonnets in the Roman dialect, most of them coarse and obscene, many of them blasphemous. He never quite learned to reconcile the conformist and rebel lious sides of his nature. Before he died at the age of 72 in 1861 he ordered his verse panorama of Roman life to be destroyed, but the order was, thanks to a liberal and far-sighted senior prelate, disobeyed. The sonnets were not published in Belli's lifetime and were known chiefly through Belli's tavern recitations of them. The Russian writer Gogol, who spent some time in Rome, heard Belli and was impressed. Sainte-Beuve in Paris heard about Belli and mentioned him in a *Causerie de Lundi*. James Joyce, the Irish novelist, who worked miserably as a bank clerk in Rome in the 1900s, seems to have read Belli, whose vast sonnet-sequence, presenting realistically the demotic life of a great capital city, may be regarded as a kind of proto-*Ulysses*. Belli can be seen as an underground link between the age of romanticism and the age of naturalism.

Giovanni Gulielmi's mother decided, in tremulous old age, that she would leave Rome and die in England. Gulielmi took her back overland on a long and painful journey. When they reached Manchester in 1832 she was not quite ready for death, but her son reserved a plot for her in Moston Cemetery. Meanwhile, forty years old, he fell in love with Sara Higginbotham, the daughter of a Manchester cotton broker and nearly twenty years his junior. Gulielmi sold his Italian property and bought a house of some size in Rusholme, close to Platt Fields. His mother duly died and he wrote an indifferent sonnet *in English*, extolling her virtues. He prospered as the translator of Dickens's novels into Italian, taught Italian privately, helped certain Manchester cotton houses with their Italian and French correspondence.

Mr and Mrs Gulielmi had one child only, a son named Joseph Joachim, born in 1840. Joseph Joachim was trained as a singer at the Manchester Royal College of Music, and had a notable bass voice notably heard in performances of Handel and Mendelssohn oratorio and in sung mass at the Church of the Holy Name, Manchester, but he became best known as a private teacher of *bel canto* and pianoforte. Manchester was then, as now, a very musical city. Joseph Joachim married a Scottish lady, Ann Mackenzie, and had three children. The youngest child, Joseph John Gulielmi, worked for the United Cattle Products Company and anglicised his name to Wilson during a wave of anti-Italian feeling occasioned by alleged ice-cream poisoning in the 1890s in the Lancashire coastal resorts of Blackpool, Clevelys, Bispham and Fleetwood.

Joseph John Wilson married an Irish waitress he met in one of the U.C.P. restaurants in Manchester. This girl, six months after the marriage, gave birth to a son named for his grandfather Joseph Joachim. This boy, born in Moss Side in 1916, was to be—by a twist if not genetic then purely coincidental, since family interest in Giuseppe Gioacchino Belli was born and apparently died with the founder of the family—the translator into English of the great Roman poet. He had no linguistic endowment for the task, since Italian was no longer spoken in the family, but as a boy at St Bede's College, Manchester, he showed skill in facetious or scurrilous versifying and a passion for the Petrarchan sonnet-form. While in the Fifth Form he openly sneered in class at Wordsworth's ineptness in management of the ABBA ABBA rhyme-scheme as also at Rupert Brooke's timidity. But he praised the fearlessness of Gerard Manley Hopkins, a poet not then much read. He drew laughter from his fellow-pupils and his English teacher alike when he stoutly declared that Keats's best Petrarchan sonnet was the one on Mrs Reynolds's cat.

J. J. Wilson was himself no poet. He made a strict distinction, even as a schoolboy, between the art of poetry and the craft of verse. His approach to the craft of the Petrarchan sonnet may be seen in three versifyings of low jokes made at the age of eighteen and submitted to the school magazine. They were rejected but not before they had, by some oversight, got into galley proof.

The Bet

Some men were talking, as men often will,
About their wives. And each with each one vied.
Over his beer, with a grim sort of pride,
Saying: "Mine's ugly."—"But mine's uglier still,"
Comparing photographs. "If looks could kill,
My missis could effect mass homicide.
Just look." But one man, with no picture, cried:
"Ugly? Come home with me and feast your fill."

A bet, then? Reet. The money was not lacking,
A quid per man. Their winter breaths asmoke,
They homed with him when "Time please" sent them
      packing.
"Get ready, missis." From upstairs she spoke:
"Am I to hide me face wi' piece of sacking?"
"Nay," he called, "it's a bet, lass, not a poke."

Two Uses for Ashes

"The ashes of my dear departed?" said
The widow, serving tea and cakes at five
Five days after the funeral. "I contrive
To house them aptly. No, not lapped in lead.
See, they are in an eggtimer instead,
There on the mantelpiece. Ah, ladies, I've
Determined, since he did no work alive,
The lazy pig shall do some now he's dead."

One widow took her man's remains as snuff,
Achieving an orgasmic kind of sneeze.
She said: "The bugger's appetite was rough.
He hentered, without even saying please,
My hother hapertures. Enough's enough.
But as he's dead I'll not begrudge him these."

Privy Matters

A man sat once, writhing in costive pain,
For a whole wretched hour, crouching inside
A public W.C. And though he tried
To loose the load, his muscles limp with strain,
He could not. Yet again. Again. Again.
But no. He heard a desperate urgent stride
To the next nook. A hefty splash. He cried:
"Lucky."—"Lucky? That was my watch and chain."

There is another ending, one that I
Have in a scatographic thesis met.
The costive heard the urgent feet draw nigh,
The thunder of release immediate.
"Ah, lucky," was his sigh. But the reply:
"Lucky? I haven't got me kecks down yet."

These sonnets are juvenile and tasteless, as one might expect
from a Catholic Manchester schoolboy, but the same charges
have been made against the work of Belli himself. One ought
to note the attempt on the part of J. J. Wilson to use dialectal
elements. A Catholic provincial, aware of his foreign blood, he
never felt wholly at home in the patrician language of the
British Establishment and would, especially in exalted company, deliberately use mystifying dialect words or adopt an
exaggerated and near-unintelligible Lancashire accent. He was
a small man, with reddish-gold hair inherited from his Irish
mother, delicately, or frailly, made, shy, melancholic, heavy-
smoking. He would smoke anything, from the wild flower
called honesty to pure latakea, and his chest was weak. He
was, he said, married to smoke. He never had any other wife.

Strangely, J. J. Wilson made his first translation of Belli,
paraphrase rather, before becoming acquainted with the poet.

A student at the University of Manchester in 1937, he was present at a lecture given to the University Literary Society by the Oxford poet G—y G—n. At the discussion over biscuits and coffee afterwards, J. J. ventured a remark to the effect that certain vital human experiences, such as menstruation in women and hangover in both sexes, had never been seriously dealt with even by modern poets. G—n looked him up and down over his coffee-cup and said: "You seem to be a rather coarse and unattractive character." Stung, Wilson went home and wrote the following:

> The orchidaceous catalogue begins
> With testicles, it carries on with balls,
> Ballocks and pills and pillocks. Then it calls
> On Urdu slang for goolies. Gism-bins
> Is somewhat precious, and superior grins
> Greet antique terms like cullions. Genitals?
> Too generalised. Cojones (Español)'s
> Exotic, and too whimsical The Twins.
>
> Clashers and bells—poetical if tame.
> Two swinging censers—apt for priest or monk.
> Ivories, if pocket billiards is your game.
> I would prefer to jettison such junk
> And give them g—y g—ns as a name,
> If only G—n had a speck of spunk.

Later he was to discover that he had, by anticipation, contrived a loose English equivalent of one of Belli's more outrageous sonnets.

Wilson took a moderate bachelor's degree in English Literature together with a subsidiary qualification in Italian. The language thus came back to the family via an interest in

Petrarch. Of Belli Wilson had still heard nothing. He took a short holiday in Rome in 1938, was nearly beaten up by Fascisti when he made a "fat bacon" gesture at a portrait of Mussolini, but did not visit the Viale of Trastevere, where a statue of Belli stands. Because of his pulmonary weakness, he was rejected by the armed forces when war broke out, and he spent five years in the Ministry of Information, where his versifying talents were sporadically used for a propagandist end. He was loaned out briefly to the Ministry of Food, for which he wrote "Don't pine for a pud, make do with a spud" when flour was short and potatoes in reasonable supply, but the rhyme was rejected as possessing only a dialectal validity.

After the war J. J. Wilson, through a friend met in the American Embassy in London, was found a subsidiary post in an advertising agency on Madison Avenue in New York City. He worked and lived in Manhattan until his death in 1959. He discovered the three-volume edition of Belli's *Sonetti* (Mondadori, 1952) in Brentano's bookshop, casually opened the first volume, and was at once both horrified and fascinated by the strange appearance of Belli's language:

> *Vedi l'appiggionante c'ha ggiudizzio*
> *Come s'è ffatta presto le sscioccajje?*
> *E ttu, ccojjona, hai quer mazzato vizzio*
> *D'avé scrupolo inzino de la pajje!*

But, more than anything, it was the demented devotion to the sonnet-form that now drew him to Belli, and he saw a strenuous hobby beckoning—the translating of all the 2,279 sonnets of Belli into what he was to call "English with a Manchester accent." He needed help with the Roman dialect and had to search hard in New York, whose Italian population is mainly Neapolitan, Calabrese, Sicilian, to find a speaker and reader of Romanesco. A counatergirl in the New York office of Alitalia—Susanna Roberti—was able to help him, and, horrified and fascinated by the magnitude of his self-imposed task, he set himself to translate a sonnet every day. He did not get far. He chose those sonnets dealing with biblical subjects and managed to achieve draft translations of them all. They follow here, unedited. He died prematurely (but what, when we think of Keats, can this be made to mean?), badly slashed and cracked by hoodlums on West 91st Street, where he lived, when he was staggering home at three in the morning from a party on East 84th Street. An uneasy and unhandsome death. The person is snatched away and the goods remain. And all this is the law and constitution of nature.

I The Creation of the World

One day the bakers God & Son set to
And baked, to show their pasta-master's skill,
This loaf the world, though the odd imbecile
Swears it's a melon, and the thing just grew.
They made a sun, a moon, a green and blue
Atlas, chucked stars like money from a till,
Set birds high, beasts low, fishes lower still,
Planted their plants, then yawned: "Aye, that'll do."

No, wait. The old man baked two bits of bread
Called Folk—I quite forgot to mention it—
So he could shout: "Don't bite that round ripe red
pie-filling there." Of course, the buggers bit.
Though mad at them, he turned on us instead
And said: "Posterity, you're in the shit."

The Beastly Paradise

Animals led a sort of landlord's life
And did not give a fuck for anyone
Till man fucked up their social union
With gun and trap and farm and butcher's knife.
Freedom was frolic, roughish fun was rife,
And as for talk, they just went on and on,
Yakking as good as any dean or don,
While Adam stood there dumb, with a dumb wife.

This was the boss who came to teach them what
Was what, with harness, hatchet, stick and shot,
Bashing them to red gravy, thick and hot.
He stole their speech too, making sure he'd got
Dumb servitude—the plough; if not, the pot.
He had the last word. Nay, he had the lot.

Man the Tyrant

This furred and feathered boss of bird and brute
Assumed the god, all bloody airs and graces,
Nor deigned to look down in his subjects' faces,
Treating each creature like a mildewed boot.
He swilled, he gorged, but his preferred pursuit
Mixed sticking pigs and whipping hounds on chases,
Marches through arches, blown brass and tossed maces,
With decking Eve, that bitch, in hunter's loot.

The beasts had hunted looks, being forced to make,
Poor wretches, the bad best of a bad job
And put up with that swine—all save the snake
Who, spitting like a kettle on a hob,
Weaved at the foul shapes tyranny can take
And hissed: "I'll get you yet, you fucking snob."

Origins

A sort of interlude. Let's look at dogs.
At mastiff, Great Dane, greyhound, poodle, beagle,
The sausage hound, that yelps like a sick seagull,
Asthmatic bullpups honking hard as hogs.
Now men. Irish in bogs and Dutch in clogs,
Swarthy as turds, sharp-conked as any eagle,
The Jew and Turk. Then, trying to look regal,
Tea-slurping English, and French eating frogs.

Compare some doggy that leaps on to laps
With a prize wolfhound. Different as cheese and chalk.
In spite of this, our parish ballocks yaps
About us springing from a single stalk:
One primal bitch for pups, and one for chaps.
Did you ever hear such stupid fucking talk?

Adam

If God made man, we've no call to regret
Man's love of blood and lack of bloody sense.
God, who's all what they call omnipotence,
Meaning he'll piss the bed and prove it's sweat,
Pissed on some clay and sweated cobs to get
A statue from it, sparing no expense.
Then he took breath and blew—*Haaaa Hadam.* Hence
Man's sometimes called the Puffed Up Marionette.

In just one minute he could spout out history
And write and read great tomes as tough as Plato's.
He knew it all when first he tottered bedwards.
The names of beasts and birds—no bloody mystery.
Like a greengrocer sorting out potatoes:
"This lot is whiteboys and these here King Edwards."

Image & Likeness

Now, Brother Trustgod, Godtrust (never knew
God had a rupture. Sorry), please let me
Shove in a word. I just won't have it, see.
God made us all in his own image, did he? You
Are mad. If Paul himself, yes Saint Paul, flew
Down to agree with you, I'd tell him he
Was mad. (He was mad.) Why don't you decree
Old Nick was made in God's own image too?

O bleeding Christ and Christ's own bleeding mother,
Even if the sanctified three-hatted sod
Says what you say, it's still, my half-arsed brother,
Mad. Is God's image in greengrocer's shops
Then, in greengrocers? God, he must be a God
Of cabbages and turnip fucking tops.

About Eve

Give me a woman bare as a boiled egg,
Who'd think a brush and comb came from the divvle,
Who owns no snotrag to entrap her snivel,
Or towel or dishcloth hanging from a peg,
Who has no shoe on foot or hose on leg
Nor any of the Amenities of Civil-
Ised Life, to use the advertiser's drivel,
No jakes to thrutch in and no pot to deg,

Who will sup water but not sit in it
Nor on a chair nor underneath a roof,
Who'll never see the muckman do his duty.
Picture this little lady decked in shit
From hair to heel, then try to give me proof
That Mother Eve, Christ help us, was a beauty.

Another Point of View

But some say: Scorn her not. Remember, she,
When Adam took her, did not turn her face
But drank the dreadful fire of his embrace.
Dirty or not, without her where would we
Be? She merits homage. So, with me:
"O *ave Eva,* though full of disgrace,
We love thee as the root of all our race;
Thy sap runs in us, leaves of thy living tree."

Dirty? How do we know? Perhaps her skin
Was laved in a miraculous hygiene,
Just as the second Eve was laved within.
Not that it matters. For myself, I lean
To lauding both her sordor and her sin.
Without those to wash off, who could be clean?

Greed

Which of the seven deadly sins is worst?
Pride sneering skyward, avarice shrieking *More,*
Liplicking lust, or anger, one red roar?
No, gluttony, the fifth sin, is the first.
From Adam burst a famine and a thirst
For a wormy apple offered by a whore,
A penny pippin. God has rammed its core
Down all our throats, a canker of the cursed.

That bitch, that bastard. God, I gape aghast as
I contemplate the greed that could have cast us
Into the outer darkness—fed us, rather,
To final fire. But our ingenious master's
As quick to cancel as to cause disasters,
And to this end kindly became a father.

Original Sin

The sceptic beats his brain till dawn's first dapple
Lights him and all his books to slumber's amity.
Though he's read all from Moses to Mohamet, he
Rejects the truth of temple, mosque and chapel:
That man brought sin and death and hell to grapple
His soul in irons, condemning God to damn it. He
Set up an aboriginal calamity
Or, if you like, munched a forbidden apple.

Why why why? One song, too many singers.
Why *why?* *Why* won't unwrite the bloody book.
So let them write a new one if they must.
Why why? We want an answer. They can look
In Milo Aphrodite's clutching fingers
Or up the arsehole of Pasquino's bust.

Knowledge

Before they yielded to the devil's urging
And crunched the good-bad apple to the core,
Bare innocence was all our parents wore,
Like Jesus Christ got ready for the scourging.
After their second gorge they felt emerging
A thing called shame. So rapidly they tore
Leaves from the trees to cover what before
Had been mere taps for secondary purging.

Thus good and evil, as we must conclude,
Succeed in making rude and crude and lewd
The dumpendebat and the fhairy grot.
Else why should man and missis play the prude?
Each knew, however leafily endued,
Precisely what the other one had got.

What Might Have Been

There'd be, if Adam hadn't sold our stock,
Preferring disobedience to riches,
No sin or death for us poor sons of bitches.
Man would range free, powerless to shame or shock,
And introduce all women to his cock,
Without the obstacles of skirt and breeches,
Spreading his seed immeasurably, which is
To say: all round the world, all round the clock.

The beasts would share the happy lot of men,
Despite a natural plenitude of flies.
There'd be no threats of Doomsday coming when
Christ must conduct the dreadful last assize.
Instead, the Lord would look in now and then,
Checking our needs, renewing our supplies.

A Problem

I'm puzzled. (Bear with me, Father Superior.)
If Adam's gorging had not been the means
Of turning us to compost for the beans
—Nothing more useful, yes, but nothing drearier—
And all who issue from their dam's interior
Did not end up by pushing up the greens,
Now what would be finale to those scenes
Which start with bouts of murderous hysteria?

Ah but (you say) along with immortality
There'd be no urge to sin: remember this.
Thank you. And so—predestinate causality
And no free will (but Adam had it: yes?).
What puzzles me is: would I incur fatality
If I fell down a fucking precipice?

Holy Starvation

We sinners have to eat four times a day
Or, if we happen to be English, five.
But man unfallen would have stayed alive.
If not a single crumb had come his way.
And even if they'd served him on a tray
Boiled stones, mashed mud, garnished with poison iv-
Y, he'd survive—indeed, contrive
To thrive on shit like any flower of May.

Everyone thin, carting an empty belly
About, knowing no gustatory bliss
In wine or trout or grouse in aspic jelly;
With jam a joke and fowl farci a farce.
The tongue and teeth for talk, yes; but why this
Hole, O ye holy buggers, up the arse?

Cain 1

"Cain, where is Abel?" Silence. "Cain, Cain, where
Is Abel?" Silence. *"Cain!"* Then came Cain's cry:
"Shoving your nose in. How the fuck should I
Know where he is? Or, for that matter, care?
Am I my brother's keeper?" The high air
Darkened at this, shuddered at God's reply:
"I'll tell you where, you killer—done in by
Your knife, he's pushing up those parsnips there.

Out of my sight, start running, up and down
The whole damned earth, you damned, you cursed, and cry
Through every bloody street of every town.
Howl, you unchristian swine, your dismal tune
Hurl at the stars, then shiver in the sky,
Weep till you brim the pockholes of the moon."

Cain 2

Please don't think, Herr Professor, I intend
Defending Cain. Better than you, perhaps,
I know him, but know too the sort of lapse
Drink will induce—how it can blind and bend
And break. See Cain drunk, beckoning like a friend,
Thick stick in fist, an oiled smile on his chaps,
Wooing his brother hither. Then he taps,
Raps bone, draws blood, the swine, and makes an end.

Filthy? Oh, yes. Still, it was far from funny
Having to hear God hawking up his phlegm
To spit upon his parsnips and his honey
But not on Abel's sheep, no, not on them.
Born of the breed of men and not of mice,
Cain growled revolt then cut himself a slice.

Cain 3

Reproach him not for bidding crime begin.
Evil was what he sucked in from his mother.
The murder of his innocent young brother
Derived from something deep beneath the skin.
As two and two make four, so man makes sin.
Still, there's a nagging problem tough to smother:
How did he know when one man cracks another
With force enough he does that other in?

Think now. Before Cain played the bloody brute
No one had demonstrated death as yet.
This doctrine, then, is murderous to refute:
That murder is an impulse man first met
When his teeth met inside that juicy fruit.
What's homicide? A thing your father ate.

The Ark 1

God said to Noah: "Listen, er patriarch.
You and your sons, each take his little hatchet,
Lop wood enough to build yourselves an ark
To these specifications. Roof and thatch it
Like Porto de Ripetta ferry. Mark
Me well now. Chase each make of beast and catch it.
And catch a male or female that will match it.
Then with your victuals, zoo and wives, embark.

A flood is going to test your wooden walls,
A world's end deluge. Tivoli waterfalls
Will seem an arc of piss in a urinal.
Ride it until you sight a rainbow. Then
Jump in the mud and make things grow again
Till the next world's end. (That one will be final.)"

The Ark 2

Elephants, fleas, cows, lions, sheep, wolves, hares,
Foxes and flies, roosters and stags and stallions,
Mice by platoons and rabbits by battalions,
Donkeys and pigs and bugs, monkeys and mares.
Meat by the ton, cheese, pasta, worms, figs, pears,
Maize, clover, hay, whey, pigswill, skilly, scallions,
Bones, birdseed, bran, melons like golden galleons,
Minced heart for owls and honey for the bears:

These and much more poor Noah stowed in the boat
That God made airtight, cosy, close and dark.
A year and more this barnyard was afloat,
Heady with gorgonzola, goat and skunk.
How did he cope, our blessed patriarch?
Ask him. He may respond by getting drunk.

Noah on Land

Drunk, yes. Near his palazzo, safe on shore,
Noah planted vines and fondly watched them sprout,
And when he saw the luscious grapes fill out
(One bunch weighed ten or twenty pounds, or more),
He crushed the juice in ferment, let it pour
Down the red lane, and gave a toper's shout:
"It's good, it's *fucking* good!" His drunken bout
First made him high and, after, hit the floor.

That was strong stuff, he was not used to it.
Like all us drunkards, snoring at the sun,
He lay as flat as a five-lira bit.
But—shame—our patriarch had no breeches on
And—but I'd better quote you Holy Writ—
"Displayed his balls and prick to everyone."

Age

If it is true, as the priests say it is,
That every ancient patriarch and prophet
Took a long time for old age to kill off (it
Was, in some cases, nine damned centuries),
They must have been damned short of maladies—
No stone, hard chancre, or bronchitic cough. It
Could be they postponed their trip to Tophet
With secrets still unsold in pharmacies.

Such agelessness would wreck our modern age.
That lad, see, fifty years in his high chair,
A hundred more at school, would choke with rage
(Himself a dad now, in or out of matrimony)
Waiting for dad to die and bless his heir,
Trying to run up bills against his patrimony.

The Tower

"We'd like to touch the stars," they cried, and, after,
"We've *got* to touch the stars. But how?" An able-
Brained bastard told them: "Build the Tower of Babel.
Start now, get moving. Dig holes, sink a shaft. A-
Rise, arouse, raise rafter after rafter,
Get bricks, sand, limestone, scaffolding and cable.
I'm clerk of works, fetch me a chair and table."
God meanwhile well-nigh pissed himself with laughter.

They'd just got level with the Pope's top floor
When something in their mouths began to give:
They couldn't talk Italian any more.
The project died in this linguistic slaughter.
Thus, if a man said: "Pass us that there sieve,"
His mate would hand him up a pail of water.

Lot 1

Two strangers, both with staffs, but one a bit
Lame from the journey, weary but still wary,
Came at the holy hour of the Hail Mary
(I love anachronising Holy Writ)
Looking for lodgings. Lot, who had just lit
His lamp, saw them, called them and said: "You're very
Welcome here." They smiled: "Ah, a *good* fairy.
Such kindness. You'll be amply paid for it."

These two were angels. The buggers of Gomorrah,
Hearing of their arrival, knew it not,
Else all their hair would have stood up in horror.
Their pricks stood up instead. They yelled out: "You
Selfish unsodomite, let's have them, Lot.
You don't require their arses, and we do."

Lot 2

The angels now announced themselves to Lot
And said "This town must suffer for its fault.
No rooftop, cavern, hole or nether vault
Will hide them when the flames leap high and hot.
You and your family leave now. Do not halt
And look back down Longara Road. *Do not,*
We say again." But hardly had they got
Away when Lot's wife turned and turned to salt.

Ah, woman, cursed by curiosity.
If all of our Italian women could
So change, as by that precedent they should,
They'd soon destroy the salt monopoly
And bring the price down, though of course we would
Be forced to live on salt and sodomy.

Lot 3

God, then, assumed the office of a cook
And baked the Sodomites like salmon trout.
Only the family of Lot got out,
Though his wife suffered for that backward look.
They camped near Zoar, in a stony nook.
Lot's daughters, starved of love, began to pout,
Seeing no sign of penises about,
And, driven by a fleshly need, forsook

Propriety. Here at least was their father.
They gave him wine with a well-salted pasty.
When he was drunk they fucked him to a lather,
Not finding this unnatural or nasty.
No fire rained down. It seems that God is rather
Inclined to incest but hates pederasty.

Abraham I

The Bible, sometimes called the Jewish Chronicle,
Says, midway between Noah's and Aaron's ark,
That Abraham played the grand old patriarch
And sacrificed to God, with fine parsonical
Language that all that blood made sound ironical.
He took a donkey from the donkey-park
(Chewing up chicory and grass in stark
Lordly disdain, as if it wore a monocle)

And called to Isaac: "Pack the bags and load
This ass here, get the boy to bring a nice
Sharp axe, then kiss your mother on the cheek.
Bring coats and hats, we're going to take the road.
The blessed Lord requires a sacrifice.
The time has come to teach you the technique."

Abraham 2

They ate, while day was cooking in the east,
Some breakfast. When their journey had begun,
Abraham led them in an orison
That lasted for a hundred miles at least.
Then the old swine or, if you wish, old priest
Said: "We've arrived. Shoulder that burden, son.
And as for you—" (meaning the other one)
"—Wait here. You too," he told his fellow-beast.

They started climbing. Halfway through their climb,
Isaac said: "Where's your victim wandered to?"
"Wait," said his father. "All in God's good time."
They reached the top, where knife-edged breezes blew,
And Abraham said: "A victim, yes. Well, I'm
The priest, son, and there's only me and you."

Abraham 3

"No, no!" The boy knelt in his innocence
—The right position for that butcher-dad
Who raised his axe above the hapless lad,
Ready to do paternal violence.
"Stop!" cried a voice. "I think we can dispense
With filicide." An angel. "You've just had
A Godsent test, and passed it, I might add.
Baaaah—here's a sheep. Quite a coincidence."

To cut it short (I'm sick of the damned story),
The sheep was slain, and all the four went home,
The ass to pasture, Isaac to his mother.
As for the slab he nearly made all gory,
It's a prized relic, hidden safe in Rome,
At Borgo-novo, or some place or other.

Joseph 1

Some merchants, so it's said, near signed the pledge and
Gave up the drink when they heard something odd:
A yell deep in a well. "A child, by God,"
One said, sticking his chin over the edge and
Peering. They hired a dredger then to dredge and
He dredged up, dripping like a landed cod,
Howling like hell, a stinking clayey clod,
Joseph the Jew, so goes the ancient legend.

They dried him, cleaned him, gave him fodder and
Bought him a shirt against the inclement weather,
But didn't want to bring him up by hand.
Seeking returns on what they'd clubbed together
They sold him off in Egypt, contraband,
For a few rags and half a trank of leather.

Joseph 2

Joseph grew up. When he was fully grown,
The lady that he worked for cast him looks
Whose drift he thought he'd read about in books,
Sighing, trying to get him on his own.
She ogled him with many a meaning moan,
Carefully careless with her eyes and hooks.
Her hunger could not be assuaged by cooks,
Only by some raw mutton with no bone.

One morning, bringing the hot water to her,
He found her naked, the sweet buxom slut,
So damped her with the contents of the ewer.
She grabbed him by his single garment but
He left it with her, naked but still pure,
And ran away, the bloody idiot.

Exodus

Pharaoh, a rogue in charge of other rogues,
First drowned the Jews then turned them into slaves,
Driven to toil by knaves with stones and staves,
Just where the fertile Nilus disembogues.
But Moses (the humane dictator vogue's
Said to start here), after some narrow shaves,
Led the Jews out between two walls of waves:
The buggers didn't even wet their brogues.

When the Red Sea swung open like a door,
The Jews assumed their journey was near done,
Not having met the love of God before.
But round and round beneath the desert sun
They had to frig for forty years and more—
A fucking waste of time for everyone.

Balaam's Ass

As ancient Hebrew story tellers knew
The future better than the past, we lack
Proof that when Balaam rode his donkey's back
And, since it halted, beat it black and blue
The poor beast turned on him and brayed: "Hey, you,
Why did you launch that unprovoked attack?
If you could see that angel there you'd thwack
This ass, or arse, more gently than you do."

If you believe this, welcome an incursion
Of awe to learn that donkeys can be pat in
High-class Italian (English in this version).
Accept the premise and it follows that in
Pointing you out the donkeys that know Latin
(*Aspeeeerges meeeeee*) I cast no foul aspersion.

The Battle of Gideon

300 Jews knitted their warlike brows and,
Armed with trombones and torches hid in skillets,
Marched in good order on their foemen's billets,
Quiet as a moving munching herd of cows. And
As dancers on the stage taking their bows and
Boos in an endless belt endlessly fill it, s-
O this small troop marched in a circle till its
300 men looked damned near like 3000.

Ta-rah, ta-ray—clash pans, flash torches. Flustered,
And deafened as 300 brass are mustered,
The enemy collapses like a custard.
Such thrift! Today we have our martial brawls,
Our soldiers heed the bugle when it calls
And waste 300 fucking cannon-balls.

Foxes

The Bible is quite verminous with foxes.
Samson caught hundreds and, with foxy cunning,
Tied torches to their tails and set them running
Through his foes' harvest-fields—thus, with hot proxies,
Saving them sweat. Still, they wished ninety poxes
Upon him and increased their vengeful gunning.
Where are the foxes now? It seems they're shunning
Our hounds as we shun syphilitic doxies.

We ought to want them, since they stank of virtue
When Samson used them against naughty men.
But still an eggless henless world would hurt you
More than a foxless. If he came back again
With scores of foxes sniffing round his skirt, you
Would say: "I'd rather have a fucking hen."

Revenge 1

Of all the Bible stories that they tell,
This one to come is quite the most fantastic.
A sonnet being so damned inelastic,
I'll require two to tell it really well.
Well, now—the exodists from Egypt's hell
Met the mad Malechites who, dreadful, drastic,
Ferocious, tastelessly enthusiastic,
Fell on the Hebrews, and the Hebrews fell.

God made a memorandum. After all,
The Jews pursued the then correct religion.
After four hundred years he called on Saul.
"The Malechites," he said, "deserve the axe.
Spit the whole nation; roast it like a pigeon.
Don't leave a feather on their fucking backs."

Revenge 2

So in God's name Saul went and waded in,
Trouncing them in one horrible stampede,
Goats, calves and all. Mercy maybe or greed
Or something made him save Prince Agag's skin.
Samuel now prophesied about Saul's sin!
"Idolater, betrayer of our creed,
A holier Israelite will supersede
Your reign and make a holier reign begin.

Bring me the prince you blasphemously spared."
Tremulous as a fatted pig, that prince
Stuttered—agag agag aghast, shit-scared.
The holy Samuel did not blink or wince
But raised the butcher's blade that he had bared
And made a mound of Malechitish mince.

David 1

How powerful is God's arm! He sent a boy
To fight Goliath, who was tough and scary,
Who swallowed foes like oysters of the prairie
And thought he'd stamp on David like a toy.
But God wished Israel to yell with joy
To know that every flabby, weak, unhairy
Weed that loves Jesus and his mother Mary
Finds giants rather easy to destroy.

Seeing the stone and sling and stripling shepherd,
Goliath cried: "You little prick, you've gone a
Mite too far," and tensed up like a leopard.
But David blessed the saints and the Madonna,
Measured his fireline, fired his pebble up it
And saw Goliath crumple like a puppet.

David 2

King David's later life? The stories vary.
It seems, though, his prophetic eye was sharp,
He spoke with God, he much preferred the bar-p-
Arlour to the coffee-shop or dairy.
Jesus, of David's seed through holy Mary,
For David was a very pericarp,
Had his gab-gift, but could not play the harp
Nor sing like David, King Saul's prize canary.

The Bible gives a fairish bona fide
Account of him, although it's hard to follow:
The story is elliptical, untidy.
You'll learn, however, that he loved to wallow
In love, and frot until his balls were hollow,
From Saturday till pretty late on Friday.

Wisdom

Solomon's judgment. So. It makes you laugh.
But could a judge upon a modern bench,
Nose lifted high against the rabble's stench,
For all his wigs and tomes and courtroom staff,
Do better? He, drained like his own carafe,
Hearing one wench scream at the other wench
In language that would make a bargee blench,
Could only say: "Let's chop the child in half."

The parish register was plain to see,
You say. He could have checked on her or her name,
The date and place of birth of son or daughter.
Fool. In those days nobody had a surname,
And parish registers came in A.D.,
When Christ had shown a brand-new use for water.

Judith

The Holy Bible tells how the seduc-
Tive Judith feasted Holofernes, winner
Of the late bloody war. They finished dinner,
She doused the lights. He, leering at his luck,
Leapt on her unresisting. Then she struck
His head off with a sword and cried: "Foul sinner,"
(His milk still frothing to the boil within her)
"Now you can find some blacker hole to fuck."

She heaved the head up in her lily hand,
Though it was heavy, horrible and gory,
And did a tour of triumph through the land.
I find two morals in this sacred story:
(a) Prove your faith by killing people and
(b) Be a bloody whore for heaven's glory.

Susannah

The chaste Susannah—what was she chased for?
Her beauty, yes, but was there something more?
The sort of reputation that she bore?
You said the word, not I: the word is w—e.
Those old men said it too (Ach, nothing's lower
Than watching at a lady's bathroom door).
But Daniel caught them out. His lion-roar
Condemned their heads, not hers, to hit the floor.

Chaste, was she? Hm. Perhaps she couldn't bring
Herself to fancy two limp bits of string.
A woman's nature's nature-in-the-spring.
To get to know it, cease your pondering,
Slap on your chest two puddings in a sling
And let your haunches launch into a swing.

Belshazzar's Feast

Belshazzar, drunk, observed a kind of smoke
Resolve itself to something vaguely manual
Writing upon the wall. He called on Daniel.
"*Many tickle your arse*— What's this—a joke?"
The ambiguous bilge that Daniel then spoke
Made less sense than the yapping of a spaniel.
"Weighed in the balance to the utmost granule,
Found wanting." Why not just "You're going to croak"?

All right, that's not a literal translation.
But what came next was no big fat surprise:
Belshazzar didn't live to eat his breakfast.
A prophet, scared of sticking out his neck, fast-
Idious about his reputation,
Ought to be told that riddles are damned lies.

II Dec. 8

Serious talk now; let's not arse about.
December eight—what do we celebrate?
Come on, you know. Good—the Immaculate
Conception. When that apple-loving lout
Adam first took it in his head to flout
The Lord's law, angels said: "Evacuate,"
And firmly locked the paradisal gate,
Keeping his maculate descendants out.

Poor Mother Nature, ever since that ban,
Cannot breed even half a child that's blameless.
There boils within the rising prick of man
The seed of something terrible though nameless.
So praise to Joachim who, with Saint Ann,
Achieved a fuck that was uniquely shameless.

Annunciation

You know the day, the month, even the year.
While Mary ate her noonday plate of soup,
The Angel Gabriel, like a heaven-hurled hoop,
Was bowling towards her through the atmosphere.
She watched him crash the window without fear
And enter through the hole in one swift swoop.
A lily in his fist, his wings adroop,
"Ave," he said, and after that, "Maria.

Rejoice, because the Lord's eternal love
Has made you pregnant—not by orthodox
Methods, of course. The Pentecostal Dove
Came when you slept and nested in your box."
"A hen?" she blushed, "for I know nothing of—"
The Angel nodded, knowing she meant cocks.

Enter Joseph

Only a few weeks after did our Virgin see
The need to make a matrimonial match,
To build a nest wherein the egg could hatch
(Her little belly had begun to burgeon, see.)
It was, therefore, a matter of some urgency.
She didn't seek the freshest of the batch;
The one she gave her hand to was no catch,
But any port will do in an emergency.

The foolish gossips gossiped at the feast:
"She might have got a younger one at least,
Not an old dribbler frosty in the blood."
But that old dribbler dribbling by the side
Of such a beautiful and youthful bride
Found his dry stalk was bursting into bud.

The Visit

Mary received, while burning Joseph's toast,
A letter. "Who the hell—?" (under her breath),
Aloud: "It's cousin Saint Elizabeth."
Elizabeth, it seemed, could also boast
A pregnancy, though not from the Holy Ghost.
Still, her next birthday was her sixtieth.
Though travel then was slow expensive death,
"We're coming," Mary wrote, then caught the post.

They went. After a short magnificat,
The women were soon chattering away
Of swellings, morning sickness, and all that.
Joseph decided that he'd like to stay
A month or so, and so hung up his hat.
Better than sawing wood all bloody day.

The Magi

From a far country—how far? Very far:
It grows, for instance, cinnamon and cocoa—
Three kings, their robes rococo or barocco,
Followed their leader—viz., that big bright star.
Each Magus had, like any czar or tsar,
Guards, steeds, a page, a clown with painted boko,
Coaches, a camel, and in leisured loco-
Motion they swayed towards where the Hebrews are.

They reached the stable with their caravan
One morning, evening, noon or afternoon,
With gifts—incense for God, and myrrh for man.
For Christ as king they had a gold doubloon—
Proper, they thought, for the top Christian.
They were, it seems, some centuries too soon.

Circumcision

Our Lady had a painful Christmas Day
And heaven the monopoly of mirth.
Between an ox and ass she brought to birth
A stableboy that stank of rags and hay.
His substitutive dad had to obey
The Jewish law, so look the Lord of Earth
Templewards, to have half a farthingsworth
Of hypostatic foreskin cut away.

Thirty years later saw the blessed Lord on
A journey to the rolling river Jordan
To be baptised by Mary's cousin's son.
A Christian man thus sprang from a prepuceless
Jew. I call most turncoats fucking useless
But make a rare exception for this one.

The Living Prepuce

That sacred relic, by the way, was hid
And either kept in camphor or else iced.
It grew so precious it could not be priced.
And then one day His Holiness undid
A holy box and raised a holy lid—
Behold—the foreskin of our saviour Christ,
Shrimplike in shape, most elegantly sliced,
At last to profane eyes exhibited.

In eighty other Christian lands they show
This self-same prize for reverent eyes to hail.
You look incredulous, my friend. But know
That faith, though buffeted, must never fail.
The explanation's this: God let it grow
After the clipping, like a fingernail.

The Slaughter of the Innocents I

Joseph was doing bull-roars on his back,
A dream corrida crowd was yelling "Toro!"
He slept cut off from coming care and sorrow,
Making the stable shake with roar and rack.
But then an angel dealt him a rough smack
And said: "You know what day it is tomorrow?
The twenty-eighth. I managed, see, to borrow
A copy of the current almanac."

Herod announced the Feast of Childermass.
Joseph rushed out and had to pay a pretty
Price (how he cursed) for an old spavined ass:
A carpenter would rather gyp than be gypped.
And so they moved off mouselike towards Egypt,
Missing a lively day in David's city.

The Slaughter of the Innocents 2

King Herod now, to minimal applause,
Ordered the babies to be stuck like swine.
There was an uproar then in Palestine
And not, O Jesus help us, without cause.
Those who had seen this coming did not pause
To hide their babes, but let them croon or whine
As visible as laundry on the line,
While they had masses said to Santa Claus.

Their saviour (saviour?) halfway to the delta
Smelt nothing of the filthy bloody welter
Nor heard the parents curse or ululate.
The troops of Herod smote and did not spare
But with each crack a splinter sought the air
And feebly tapped on heaven's heavy gate.

Baptism

When he was old enough for politics
Jesus went splashing on the Jordan's bed.
He ceased to be a Jew and joined instead
The Apostolic Roman Catholics.
Then he went dropping homilies like bricks.
"He who seeks heaven with an unwashed head
Will see the kingdom with his arse," he said,
Shouting the odds, wagging his crucifix.

Only his mother got there unbaptised,
Which proves she waved goodbye to mother earth
A good Jewess, staunch in the faith and steady.
Heaven had got her soul well organised:
Why rub and scrub a thing that came to birth
As white as someone's laundry line already?

A Wedding at Cana I

The guests at Cana, vinously aswim,
Aroar for more, found every bloody butt
Was empty, and the liquor stores were shut.
The innkeeper, fired by a roguish whim,
Had three casks filled with water to the brim,
Then told each sozzled fuddled serving slut
To lug them where, importantly astrut,
The host was, and to leave the rest to him.

Christ was a guest, dressed in his best apparel,
But the host begged a sort of magic act
Through Mary: "Make him turn this lot to wine."
Mary replied: "I know this son of mine—
Moody. But if I speak to him with tact
You'll get, maybe, a quarter of a barrel."

A Wedding at Cana 2

And so she begged an instant grapeless wine,
But Jesus, who was hardly yet adult,
Sighed like a stone leaving a catapult
And scowled: "This problem's neither yours nor mine,
Mother. Permit me coldly to decline
To help these boozers. Easy or difficult
Is not the point. Let the fat host consult
Some other thaumaturge, the smirking swine.

Just so some soak can blurt a drunken toast
Or swill the teeth he's sunk into a roast,
You want me to work miracles and such,
To get a toothcomb and go combing out
The various troubles lurking all about.
I've troubles of my own, thanks very much."

A Wedding at Cana 3

Jesus, I think (Christ rest his spirit), chose a
Tantrum like that one not to be unkind
But to show off. A young man is inclined
To blow his trumpet oftener than his nose. A-
Las, Our Lady, so says the composer
Of this instructive rhapsody, repined.
She'd had maternal victory in mind
But now became the Mater Dolorosa.

I sometimes wish this story had not happened;
But heed its lesson, if you heed no other:
Try not to be the big loud man too soon.
God heard the answer that he gave his mother,
Determined on a right reproving rap and
Lathered his arse one Friday afternoon.

Anger

Jesus forgives all sins—or nearly all:
Usury, anger, greed, the knife thrust under
The ribs, robbery, calumny, lying, plunder
Of land condoned by rogues in the town hall.
Only on one occasion did he fall
Into a rage that tore him near asunder
And made him roar with true Jehovan thunder
And bounce in bloody anger like a ball,

And that was when he saw the Church done wrong to.
He took a whip with many a knotted thong to
The moneychangers preying on those praying at
                    the temple.
This is the only place in Holy Writ
Where Christ is shown as throwing a mad fit.
He aged with righteous rage and started greying at
                    the temple.

Martha & Mary

Martha said: "Christ, I'm full up reet to' t' scupper
Wi' Mary there." She belted out her stricture:
"Rosaries, masses—it fair makes you sick t'your
Stomach. Stations o' t' Cross. I'm real fed up. A
Carthorse I am, harnessed neck and crupper
While she does nowt. About time this horse kicked you
Right in the middle of your holy picture,
Mary. Go on, now. Say it: *What's for supper?*"

"Martha, O Martha," sighed the blessed Saviour,
"You've no call to get mad at her behaviour.
She's on the right road, and you're out of luck."
"The right road, aye," said Martha. "Why, if I
Went on like her, this house would be a sty,
And she'd not see the right road for the muck."

Communion

With the Last Supper finished and the waiter
Ready to clear, Christ took a loaf of bread,
Blessed it, then fed it to the already fed,
Making each eater a communicator.
He even gave some to his darling traitor,
Proving his mood was rosy, not yet red
(Judas Iscariot, who lost his head
And went to play at swings a little later).

But, friendly as he was, the Master knew
His passion hour was coming, hot and hellish,
So made a good confession, to embellish
His church with not one sacrament but two.
There then remained one holy thing to do—
To eat himself, with little or no relish.

Christ & Pilate

After they'd knotted Jesus up with rope,
Judas assisting, damned and dirty dastard,
After the high priest's bullies, who had mastered
The spitting art, had given it full scope,
After the maids and grooms had heard the Pope
Say: "I don't give a fuck about the bastard",
They led our Lord to Pilate's alabastered
Hand-washing room, already sweet with soap.

This was a case Pilate could not refuse.
He saw the filth of it but might not shed it—
A swine, yes, but a clean swine, to his credit.
He said: "You're Jesus, then, king of the Jews?"
Christ sought not to deny, affirm or edit,
But looked him in the eye and said: "You've said it."

At the Pillar I

Bare as a Briton auctioned into slavery,
Lashed to a post, Jesus, from head to feet,
Beaten by bastards who knew how to beat,
Yielded his skin to graduates in knavery.
No spot was spared. He ended an unsavoury
Blue-green-vermilion chunk of dirty meat,
The sort that's bought for cats and dogs to eat
From fly-buzzed butchers' barrows in Trastevere.

No spot spared? Well, I did some small research
Into that very whipping post, that's placed,
As is well known, in St Prassede's church,
And found it didn't come up to my waist.
So, though Christ's limbs, loins, face, flanks, belly shared
Foul blows, his sitteth-on-God's-right was spared.

At the Pillar 2

You've seen a felon in the public pillory
Having his buttocks beaten to a mash,
And much admired his cool disdainful dash,
The muscles firm—both gluteal and maxillary
(Aided no doubt by draughts from the distillery).
But now consider Christ beneath the lash,
Deafened by the incessant crash and slash
Of leather, sticks, the whole damned crude artillery.

Consider how each whipstroke gashes, galls
Ribs, shoulders, flanks, how bits of torn flesh keep
Falling away, as, say, boiled mutton falls
From the bone. But does the victim whine or weep?
No. Though all that is left him is his balls,
He merely counts the strokes, like counting sheep.

Pity

How can you think of Christ without a sob?
Dropped like a beast in a foul nest of straw,
Forced, as a boy, with hammer, pliers, saw
To slave away at a woodworker's job,
A youth, he walked the world with grumbling maw,
Preaching the word to a disdainful mob,
A man, he had a price upon his nob,
And Judas sold him to the Roman law.

The spit, the lash, the doom, the thorny crown,
The nails, the cross, the vinegar-soaked rag
Tied to a pole, the diced-for bloody gown:
All burdens fell upon him, sacred bag
Of bones—hence the old saying handed down:
Flies always settle on a spavined nag.

Two Kinds of Men

We come into this world bedecked in shit,
Some of us anyway, including Jesus.
But others are born rich as fucking Croesus,
Mightily proud, mightily proud of it.
The crown, the coronet, the mitre fit
Men for whom earth gushes out gold like geysers,
While we are lemons ready for the squeezers,
Scarred nags for spurs, bare backsides to be hit.

If Christ was one of us, why did he give in
Such plenty palaces for those to live in,
Making us stew in filth and sweat and pus?
Why, even on the cross, in the last flood
Of pain, it was for them he gushed forth blood
But trickled bloody water out for us.

Guilt

There's a whole race that seems to merit hell
Because the bloody reprobates refuse
To join the Church of Rome—I mean the Jews.
They let Christ die upon the cross as well.
Still, as some learned Jewish rabbis tell,
There is a circumstance that one may choose,
If one's fair-minded, that can near-excuse
The dozen errant tribes of Israel.

When Christ went to fulfil his métier,
He knew Good Friday was his destined day:
Death was a big word in his lexicon.
Doomed-to-be-slain (put it another way)
Must meet a complementary doomed-to-slay.
Somebody had to take that business on.

Limbo

When Jesus rose triumphant from the tomb,
Defying natural law as well as Roman,
He whizzed down like a shot shot by a bowman
And dragged the holy souls from Limbo's gloom.
Then Purgatory started to assume
The place of rhubarb in a sick abdomen;
Masses were sold like tickets by a showman—
Twin innovations that are still in bloom.

The angels, after brooding wings akimbo,
Put infant souls, baptised in milk and piss
But not the font, into that empty Limbo.
It wasn't meant to last, of course, and when
The Last Trump offers only blaze or bliss,
Christ knows where the young bastards will go then.

Christ in Hell

The Creed says Christ descended into Hell.
What could his Father have been thinking of,
Sending him there? Is that paternal love?
Jesus in Hell. Christ Jesus. Hell. Well, well,
For my part faith and candour both compel
My stating that the buggers up above—
Not God but government—desired to shove
Christ in that ill-appointed hot hotel.

Jesus in Hell. O Jesus Christ in Hades.
Ever since earth was earth and sky was sky,
A finer gentleman, gentlemen, ladies,
Was never picked to whip and crucify
Than Jesus. Let's believe that when he made his
Trip it was just hello and then goodbye.

Doubt

When Christ rose up, those somewhat timid gentry
His friends kicked up a noise, but one apostle
—St Thomas—sang as loud as any throstle:
"It's an imposture. Obvious. Elementary.
Anyway, how could he pass the fucking sentry?"
Jesus meanwhile, unseen in the Easter jostle,
Was making for their place at a colossal
Speed, and he used the keyhole for his entry.

He cried: "Poke in your finger, near this rib,
And you'll soon see whether I still exist
Or the whole tale is just a fucking fib."
St Thomas came and shoved his great ham fist
Into the hole. He then became as glib
A Christian as he'd been a rationalist.

Whitsun

You've seen the cook shove larding needles in
Pork, lamb, beef or some other meaty treat,
While seated on your trattoria seat,
Hungry as hell and anxious to begin.
Fat spits and bubbles underneath the skin,
The very sizzle's good enough to eat,
And while the flame and fat and fibre meet,
Saliva dribbles almost to your chin.

This is one way to cook a fine fat pigeon,
But not the dove of pentecostal peace.
Dressed as a grilled lamb-tongue, this fluttered down
And, to feed hungry bellies with religion,
It cooked the eleven apostles good and brown
Until they spat with holy grace or grease.

Spread the Word

When Jesus died, firm in the Christian creed,
St Peter's party picked up the Lord's load
And, staff in fist, they took the Cassia road
And went about the world to sow their seed.
Some sought—lazy, or fired to feed a need—
Baccano and La Storta; others strode
To Nepi, Monterosi, where they showed
The Christian way of death in word and deed.

Nay, more—to teach the good and ban and banish
The bad, they went to lands where pagans chatter
In Russian, German, English, French and Spanish.
Their message was so simple, strong, unkillable,
The fact they spoke Italian didn't matter.
No one misunderstood a single syllable.

The Last Days

When the long annals of the earth are done
And Christ's creation's melted into shit,
The Antichrist will crawl out of his pit
And preach the dirty word to everyone,
Cursed with a wall-eye that the blest will shun,
A giant body and a face unfit
Even to have tomatoes hurled at it,
A prodigy, son of a monk and nun.

The prophet Enoch will lambast the liar,
Elijah too—they'll spring out of a hatch
In St Paul's church, between the nave and choir.
Satan will slither up from hell to snatch
His share, snarling it out with the Messiah.
And earth will be a plucked up cabbage patch.

The Last Judgment

At the round earth's imagined corners let
Angels regale us with a brass quartet,
Capping that concord with a fourfold shout:
"Out, everybody, everybody out!"
Then skeletons will rattle all about
Forming in file, on all fours, tail to snout,
Putting on flesh and face until they get,
Upright, to where the Judgment Seat is set.

There the All High, maternal, systematic,
Will separate the black souls from the white:
That lot there for the cellar, this the attic.
The wing'd musicians now will chime or blare a
Brief final tune, then they'll put out the light:
Er-phwhoo.
       And so to bed.
            Owwwwwww.
               Bona sera.